Inheritance

RAVIN TIJA MAURICE

Inheritence
Copyright 2019 by Ravin Tija Maurice

Cover Art & Interior by RMGraphX

ALSO BY RAVIN TIJA MAURICE

THE AFFLICTED SERIES
REBIRTH
IKON
INHERITANCE

CAMILLE BISHOP SERIES
PROPHECY GIRL
BELIEVER

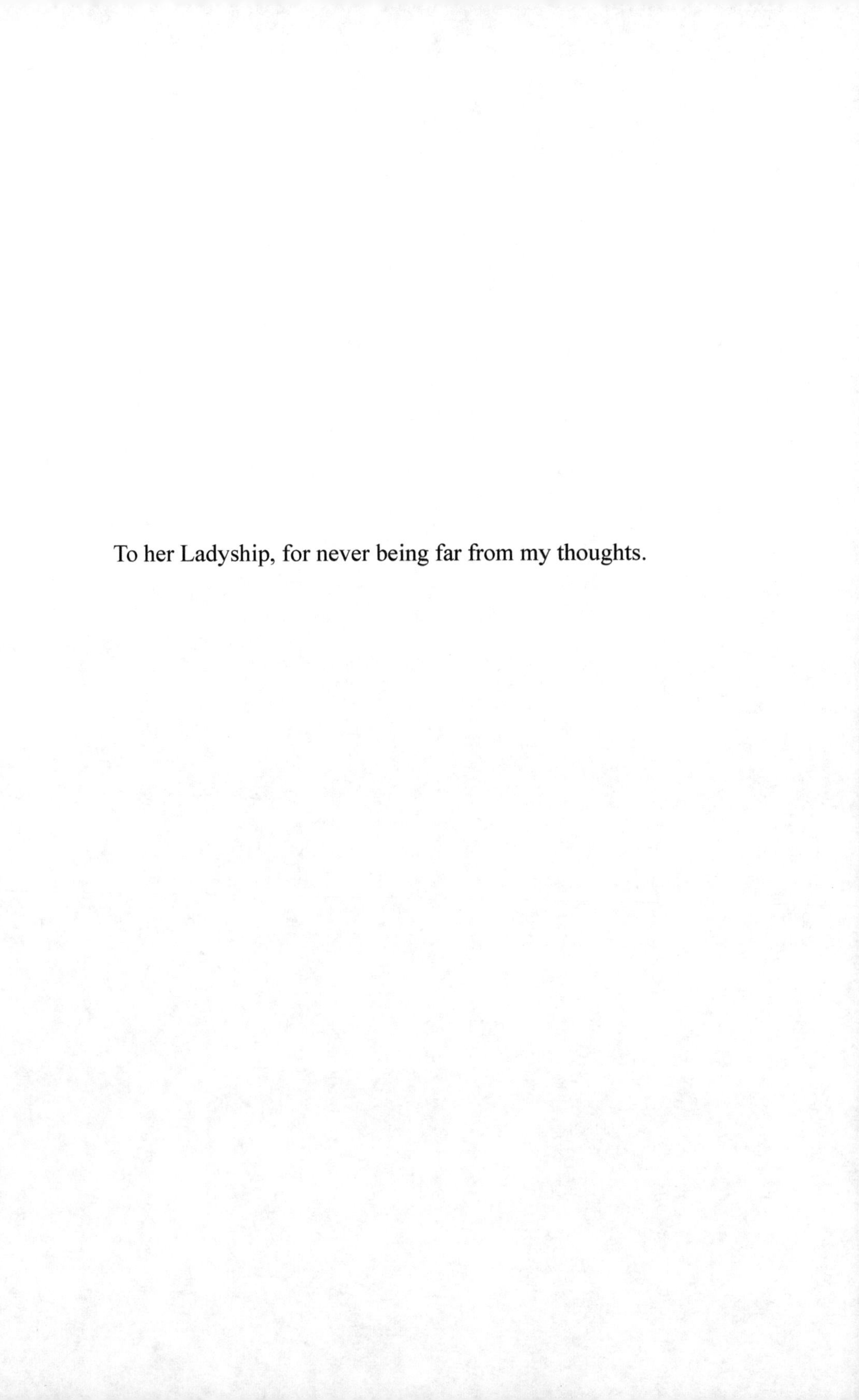

To her Ladyship, for never being far from my thoughts.

Here I stand. I can do no other
– *Martin Luther*

PROLOGUE

Grisela

"I WAS HOPING YOU WOULD COME."

She entered the room as she had done so many times before, by the large window that had been left open a crack, as if it were a hand written invitation.

The room was shrouded in candlelight, the air thick and humid. She could smell the sick when she closed the window behind her, trying to be careful not to catch her skirts.

"Bonjour, mon ami," a soft voice called out to her.

"Bonne soirée ma reine." She spoke quietly, slowly approaching the bed. She pulled a small stool over and sat, reaching out and taking the small hand that lay atop the silken covers.

"I am so pleased you could come at such short notice, cousin," the lady in the bed said, sitting up so the two could see each other better. "We must speak of a matter of some importance, Grisela. I fear I am not long for this world."

"Tell me what I can do for you, your majesty. I will do everything in my power to help," Grisela pleaded.

"Please, we are family. And I have not been queen in some time. I insist you call me Margot."

Grisela smiled. "You honour me."

"An honour you should have always received as a Valois. But soon you will be the last of us, you and your girl."

"My offer still stands, Margot. I can free you of your weakening body...."

"An offer I should have taken when I was still young if I had a mind to take it at all," she told her. "But please, allow me to continue. I fear I am not long for this world, and once I am gone I cannot guarantee your daughter's safety. She is old enough that she could finish her fostering and return home."

Grisela turned her eyes away from Margot, and the old queen smiled.

"You have not told her Father about her yet, have you?" Margot asked.

Grisela blushed. "No. I am ashamed to admit I have not. I have foolishly left it for too long. Now I am sure my loved ones will cast me out. "

"They will not! Once you explain that you were fearful of what would happen to her because of her affliction I am sure they will understand."

"Some may, and some may not. But it matters not, for it is time for Ysabeau to return to her mother's care."

Margot began to cough, a dry heave that surely made the rest of her body ache. Grisela cringed, knowing the pain that her dear cousin was in broke her heart.

Margot had believed her. When most had laughed at the idea, the great queen, la reine Margot, believed that they were related by blood.

They had met in secret for many years, and when the time came for Grisela to ask an enormous favour Margot was more than happy to oblige.

Anyone claiming to be a Valois cousin who had approached Margot previously had wanted something from her; a fortune, a title, land, all things that Margot could and would not provide.

But all Grisela had wanted was to know her.

"I am not much longer for this world, dear one," Margot confessed to Grisela. "But it warms my heart to know that you and that sweet little girl will be reunited once more and she will always remember her cousin Margot helped care for her. I saw her several months back. She is thriving and beautiful."

Grisela beamed with pride. "I am aware. She mentioned it in a letter."

"She gives me great pride and has brought me many joys, Madam. Far more then you could imagine." Margot smiled sweetly at her. "One would think that you asking me to foster her would be a burden for me. It was not. It was one of the best things I have done in this life."

"That is, perhaps, one of the most wonderful things I have ever heard. It's music to my ears."

Margot began to cough again, Grisela reached out and took her hand. Margot pressed a ring into Grisela's palm.

"So you do not forget me," she said softly.

A tear fell down Grisela's cheek. "Tell me what to do. I cannot bear to see you this way. My heart is breaking."

"Be the most remarkable mother this world has ever known. Be everything to her that our mother's were not."

"I will. And I would never forget you, Margot. You will always be la reine Margot, last and greatest of the Valois dynasty. A true queen."

Margot smiled, holding Grisela's hand tightly. "You are the last, my dear Grisela. You should call yourself Grisela Delphine du Valois; your true name, an honour you deserve."

Grisela lowered her eyes and tears began to fall down her cheeks. She had never cared for anyone as much as she loved Margot. Not her siblings, not Charles, Katrine, or even little Ysabeau. Losing her was like losing a limb; she would have to go through the process of learning to live without her as one would learn to live without an arm or a leg.

"Please do not weep for me, my dear Grisela, for I have lived much longer than I ever expected." Margot told her proudly. "I have had a full and fascinating life. Sometimes sad, sometimes happy, but never dull. No one can say that Marguerite de Valois did not *live*."

"I am crying because I will miss you so. I don't know what I will do without you, Margot," Grisela told her, looking in her crystal blue eyes. The shine that had always radiated back, even from their first meeting many years before, was beginning to dull. Grisela knew what that meant.

"I will let my people know that you will be sending for Ysabeau, my hope is that they will bring her to Paris to help ease the transition," Margot replied.

"Thank you."

"I hope to make one more public appearance. Will you come? We will not be able to interact but I would find comfort knowing you are present."

"Of course, my queen. I would be honoured. You will see me, as you have many times before, in the crowd."

THE RECOVERY

He gave me a ring, a perfect round circle to symbolise our everlasting love, made of small red stones.

Everlasting love sealed in blood.

It was comforting.

When we returned home from Russia my Grandmother's death was confirmed; a Palatine in Hungary named Thurzo decreed her name should never be spoken in polite society again.

Gabriel said he's a vile excuse for a man who was once her friend, her husband's friend. Gabriel even wondered if Thurzo had wished to marry her after Ferenc Nadasdy died.

I cared not for the particulars; he had once known all of these people rather well so the affect was different. I only wished for Thurzo to suffer as he had made her, he being the one who arrested her all that time ago.

She had trusted Gabriel, loved him even. And even though I did not at that moment I believed his reassurances that there would be justice for Erzsebet Bathory in the end. How it would come about, I did not know.

But it was comforting.

Russia had changed us all. Made life as we knew it very different, we were all cautious now and almost always on alert for danger. My beloved Gigi was now fierce and proudly defiant, I believed she was determined to show the world she was the most powerful and ruthless Delphine on earth. Her short temper and aggression now becoming notorious, I could see how she would have commanded attention as a courtesan.

Vincenzo tried to coax the softer Gigi out but that was now reserved only for those she truly cared for, which was fewer then I had thought.

But even though life was different, the Danse Macabre went on.

We danced, worked, existed while waiting for what could possibly happen. The Order of the Dragon had gone quiet; I wondered if it was because of my threat of they thought we may kill Gabriel.

"They are losing control of their members. We are the least of their worries," Gigi said. "Or perhaps they have moved on, thinking you are a lost cause."

"Moved on to whom? That is what I am worried about." I tried to hide my concern.

"You worry too much, ma petite." Gigi responded the same way to many of my concerns. I asked Morgana almost daily if she had seen anything, my own visions seeming to have run their course.

"You're looking for trouble. I thought you would be happy things had calmed and returned to normal," my Scottish friend would say.

"I've become used to trouble. This is not normal for me," I told her and she would laugh. She was right, though I refused to say it out loud.

The New Year came and I put all thought of troubles out of my mind.

Whatever came, I would face it. I could face it.

William had begun coming to the dance rehearsals, since we

returned I had thrown myself into the work and was now being featured more frequently. I felt freedom when I danced that I was sure I would not feel anywhere else in my life.

But while the stage gave me a chance to be free the two things that would control my existence for the foreseeable future sat just as I stepped off.

Gigi slammed her cane on the stage, snapping me back to reality. She had taken on the job of director since Charles had become entranced with his new pet. I hated to refer to Natalia as a pet, she was a lovely girl, but the novelty of her being a skinwalker had not worn off and Charles was so determined to keep her with us he was treating her like royalty.

So, my mentor's command of my day to day activities grew larger, and I was only slightly relieved that she treated all the dancers the same even though the other's expected her to favour me.

I turned my eyes to William's smiling face out in the seats; it was either my mentor or the man who wished to be my husband. I loved him dearly but had no wish to be controlled more then I already was.

"I hope he is not distracting you, Katrine," Gigi proclaimed loudly.

"Perhaps he should come and join us," Mathilde teased, laughing hysterically. Vincenzo came in the back of the room and William took that as a cue to leave. Before I could say anything Gigi began thumping the cane and we returned to rehearsing.

We danced till my body ached, a type of pain that had become so familiar it actually felt good.

"You are exquisite," Sybillia said as we exited the stage together. "It is as if you were meant to dance."

"Ah, but you will be the main attraction, mon ami," I told her. "Your beauty will outshine any dancing. You will be the talk of Paris!"

Her brows lowered. "Of course! They will come in droves to gawk at the Arab! They'll wonder what you have done to get your slave to behave in such a manner."

I laughed at the absurdity. "We fed and clothed her and gave her a real home! You are no slave, my dear."

She touched my shoulder; her hand was hot through my sleeve.

"All because of you, Katrine," she said quietly to me as we stepped out into the underground.

I desperately wanted a bath, and luckily Hannah had one waiting for me when we arrived back at the chateau.

"He's been asking for you." Hannah told me flatly as she washed my hair.

"Who?" I asked.

"Your cousin. I don't know why you pretend like you do not know. He asks for you every day."

"I thought at some point you would assume I knew and would stop telling me, so I wondered if you were only telling me when someone new wishes to speak with me."

She chuckled. "No, child. Tis only your poor cousin in his cage in the basement."

"Why do you pity him? He is lucky the others did not kill him."

"I pity anyone who is a victim of their own circumstances, Katrine."

I paused, contemplating the depth of her statement.

"You are very wise, my beloved maid," I told her. "Is it perhaps you feel that you are also that sort of victim?"

"Go speak with him please. Your Grandmother would expect you to be courteous to him at the very least."

I thought about what my Grandmother had said to me the last time we spoke, her blind faith that she seemed to expect me to have also.

"Had you planned on making me feel guilty?" I asked.

"If that will get you to see him, yes. He has been driving the staff quite mad, which is not good when we are still training," she proclaimed. We had lost many servants during the attack in Russia, and finding and training replacements had been a struggle. Especially for Hannah, who had taken charge of the situation.

"We were lucky that so many of the new people were family members of those we'd lost so we avoided some major difficulties," Hannah continued. "But regardless of where they came from he should not pester them so."

"Did you tell him that?"

"I did, even though it is not my place, but he felt no need to listen to me. I wonder if they should move him to the underground if they wish him to suffer. Our basement is quite lovely."

"I thought you believed him a victim?"

"Yes, but I also understand that I am not in charge. If they intend to be cruel they should be and not waste time being half hearted." Hannah was refreshingly honest as she helped me out of the bath and wrapping me in sheets. "And when you return we need to care for your feet at Mademoiselle Delphine's insistence."

"So then I best get on with it. Help me dress quickly before anyone else comes to bend my ear."

"Tis good to finally see you, cousin," Gabriel's voice came through as soon as I stepped on the basement stairs.

"You must stop harassing the servants, Gabriel," I snapped. "We are having enough difficulties returning things to normal."

He stood and I was surprised at the physical changes in him. His body was beginning to become thin. He was quite literally starting to look like half the man he once was; Gabor Bathory, Voivode of Transylvania was almost invisible now.

"If you came to see me when I first requested it such things would not be necessary." His tone was sharp; he was clearly annoyed with me.

"I am not at your beckon call! I have a life and my own problems to deal with," I yelled. "Perhaps it would be wise to move you to the underground so you understand that this is supposed to be punishment."

He watched my face as I glared at him.

"Get on with it, will you? I have things to attend to." The bark in my voice was angry.

"Is everything alright?" he asked. He seemed unfazed by my demeanour.

"Yes. Why?"

"There has been nothing from the Order?"

"Of course not. Will you get to the point?"

"Has the Scots girl seen anything?"

"For the love of God, Gabriel..."

"This makes no sense, Katrine! How could there be all of that then just nothing?"

"Perhaps they've lost interest."

He laughed loudly; the sound seemed to shake the basement and startled me. "The Order of the Dragon does not *lose interest*, and now that we have a skinwalker and the Turkish Princess I can assure you any interest they have is *far* greater than before."

"Perhaps they feel they have lost control of their people, or they are concerned for your life."

He laughed again. "Should I be concerned? Would you kill me, cousin?"

"If I believed we were in danger I would without hesitation." My voice was flat and without emotion. His eyes lit up and he smiled.

"That is why they like you, my dearest. You have inherited the Bathory's ruthless nature," he told me. "I many not know the ways of this world we live in but *I know the Order.* They are up to something, I am sure of it."

"You worry too much, Gabriel." I turned and walked away from him. "Now, unless you have something useful to tell me stop bothering the servants. I will come see you when I can."

IN THE PRESENCE OF ROYALTY

We all stood as Victorie entered the dining room, Aseem following closely behind her. Gigi tensed where she stood and watched her friend limp across the room, the scar on Victorie's cheek no longer an angry red. I was genuinely surprised she did not cover it with cosmetics, she was using a poultice Morgana had made and it had improved its overall appearance.

"You must stop doing this," Victorie said loudly. "It is nothing to fuss over."

"Nonsense! We stand as a sign of respect," Charles smiled proudly at her. I nodded in agreement, but I did understand how she might be bothered by a room full of people standing for her.

Charles had had the already grand dining room table extended to accommodate the new additions. I was surprised we all fit comfortably in the room. Victorie took her place to the left of the head of the table where Charles sat. The rest of the table had been shifted so Natalia could sit at his right hand; she was grandly dressed in a pink satin gown, cut in the French fashion and trimmed with lace. A strand of small sized pearls around her neck seemed to make her skin glow.

When we had all sat back down Charles stood again with his wine glass in hand and my heart sank. The last time he had done this he had announced our trip to Russia. I was not sure we could take another excursion.

"All I wanted to say is that I am so happy and so proud that the Danse Macabre has been able to bounce back from a major crisis and come out stronger than ever before. I know that with Grisela directing our shows that wonderful things are in store for us!" he declared loudly, raising his glass in the air. Natalia giggled as everyone else stayed silent.

"Excuse me, my Lord, but I have a request," I said after several long moments in silence.

He nodded and I continued. "I must ask that if you intend Gabriel's imprisonment to be a punishment then would you please move him to the underground?"

"That is quite a request, Katrine. May I ask why?" Charles asked.

"He is harassing the servants, which is causing major disruptions in the training."

Charles nodded in acknowledgement. "Thank you for informing me. I will give the matter some thought before taking action."

"Thank you," I said. Before any more could be said dinner was served. I was served a separate glass of blood along with my food.

"You do not feed nearly enough, so drink and do not complain," Gigi snapped at me before I could ask questions.

The food was divine, except the bread. I wondered if the maids who Roza had taught to bake had all been killed; if they had I would never taste her bread again.

I tried to clear my mind and enjoy the candied fruits and nuts that had been served for dessert. A laugh caught my attention, and I was hit sharply with the thought I had not considered Mathilde's feelings in regards to moving Gabriel to the underground.

I smiled at her, and when she finally made eye contact she smiled back and I knew she would be alright.

I felt a sharp poke in my left arm and Gigi's sharp whisper as she said, "Feed. Now!"

I was surprised at how warm the glass was when I picked it up, the sensation was surprisingly soothing. I took a big sip of the liquid; the warm blood easily flowed through my body like it was meant to be there.

"That is much more satisfying then the tea," I said to no one in particular. I heard Vincenzo chuckle as Gigi poked my free hand with her fork.

"Goodness, Gigi, you do not need to be so tough on the girl. She's 21 years old, she is not a child." Vincenzo told her quietly.

"Were you a blood drinker at 21 years of age, Vincenzo? No? So do not comment on things you know nothing about!" Gigi remarked so loudly I felt my face flush and I desperately wanted to hide my head. "This is a crucial time in her growth; her mind could slip at any moment!"

"Stop!" I slammed my glass on the table. "This is totally unnecessary."

The table went back to being silent until the dishes were cleared. I went to stand when Gigi grabbed my hand.

"What is it now?" I asked quietly.

"Go change into something more presentable. We have an appointment," Gigi said, and I left the room without another word.

Hannah dressed me in one of my more elaborate white mourning dresses, with white and icy blue embroidery and a stiff lace collar that framed my face. I had Hannah brush my hair out and I wore it long and loose around my shoulders. William did not come to my room and we did not speak at dinner.

"Can you please tell William I am sorry and I had to go with Gigi?" I asked Hannah. "I do not think I will have a chance to."

"Of course. Whatever it is, it must be important."

Gigi and I stepped out into the night and got into our carriage.

"This all seems too familiar." I confessed. I wasn't sure she heard me.

"Don't worry ma petite. This is not a case of déjà vu. We are going

to a party so I can see someone who has been in prison for many years."
Gigi spoke quietly and kept her eyes turned towards the window.

"Who?"

"It is difficult to explain. You shall understand when we arrive."

We stepped out into the darkness along with a string of others, some of the best dressed I had ever seen in Paris. We were all heading to the front doors of a grand mansion, after a quick look around I saw that we were on the banks of the Seine.

"What is this place?" I asked quietly.

"L'Hostel de la Reine Marguerite on the Left Bank of the Seine," Gigi stated as we walked quickly to the house. I understood the name of this place but I did not understand exactly what it meant.

People smiled at us as we walked through the sitting room and into the parlour, we seemed to be unrecognised. I was genuinely surprised, considering all the years Gigi had spent at court.

Then, quite suddenly, Gigi stopped. She grabbed my wrist and pulled me back to a standing place against the wall where we had a full view of the room.

Her eyes were locked on an older woman, she was probably in her 60's, who was dressed quite lavishly in a deep blue dress with a stomacher that was heavily embroidered with tiny pearls and an intricately detailed lace collar trimmed in larger pearls that framed her face perfectly, it was so stiff and white it looked as if it was made from bones. Her sand coloured hair had some strands of white woven through it; she wore it in an elaborate updo with a jewelled band just above her hairline. I had never seen sapphires so big.

She was beautiful, even more so when she smiled. She would have been quite a beauty in her youth.

Gigi's reaction to her was unsettling; she appeared overjoyed to see her but also quite upset.

"Isn't she stunning?" Gigi's voice was soft and low. "She's younger than me, you know."

I looked at the woman then back at Gigi, quite confused. "Who is she?"

"The former Queen of France, still called Queen even though she has not been for some time," Gigi began, "and...and the last of the royal family of Valois. Her name is Marguerite, some call her la Reine Margot."

"Is she your sister?"

"I believe she is my cousin. But since my mother has never told me exactly who my father was I will never know for sure. But she is the last, regardless."

"So, let's go speak to her," I said, and she pulled me back before I could move.

"Are you mad? You cannot just walk over and start a conversation with her. She is a Queen, that is not how things work," Gigi whispered sharply.

"So we shall just stand here and stare at her?"

"I gave up all hope of trying to speak to her years ago when I was at court with her family."

"Was she Queen then?"

"No, one of her brother's was King. She married the King of Navarre, who inherited the crown of France from the last of her brothers. Her husband was the first Bourbon King."

"It sounds very complicated."

"It is, and I will explain it all to you another time. Now I need to observe her in silence."

I watched Gigi as she watched Marguerite de Valois dance, converse, and seem to thoroughly enjoy her evening. The fact that this lovely, dignified and regal but older woman was younger than Gigi was not comprehensible at that moment, and the way she would freeze when Marguerite's eyes would turn in our direction was childlike and full of innocence.

Then, when the night was coming to a close Marguerite's eyes stayed on us, as if she was trying to remember who we were. She and Gigi locked eyes and something happened, Gigi curtsied to the other woman as low as she could manage and Marguerite dipped her head in acknowledgment as she walked out of the room.

Gigi sighed loudly when she stood. "It is all I could ask for."

"Do you think she knows you?" I asked.

"I do not know. We were at court together a very long time ago. But perhaps I look like a Valois." She grinned proudly. "I've grown tired of looking like my mother."

"Can we go home now?"

"Yes, yes. Of course," she replied. I followed behind her as we made our exit.

The weather had grown cold and some snow had fallen, I was happy to be in our carriage and moving.

"Thank you for coming with me, Katrine. This really means a lot to me," Gigi said, pulling a pelt over her legs.

"I am happy to. It is an honour to join you in such an important journey. Thank you for bringing me." I pulled a pelt up close to my chest to block the cold. "I am pleased to have been able to see Marguerite de Valois as well, but I still cannot believe you are the same age."

Gigi chuckled. "We have not spent much time discussing the details of our condition, have we? My apologies, I thought the men would handle these situations. We will age slowly, if at all, and cannot be killed by traditional means. It is a blessing and a curse in many ways."

I was about to say something when she continued, "It is why my family fled, and why my mother had to retire. She will be 91 this year."

"So do we need to worry? About aging, I mean?"

"No. My mother is a vampire, so it is different for her than us. She has not aged since she was turned, and she can only be killed by cutting off her head and removing her heart. Perhaps the sun would kill her too but it would be like cooking her," Gigi explained. "My brothers, twins, died of an unknown illness when they were five years old."

"How many siblings do you have? I am sure I have asked before but I have forgotten."

"My mother gave birth to ten children, only the twins died young. But only four are like me, the first three are mortals."

"Are the younger ones all like...," I began, but before I could say her name out loud Gigi silenced me with a wave.

"Somewhat. But we will not speak of that now. Thank you again, ma petite. Please keep this trip to yourself."

RETURN, LITTLE RAT

"This bread tastes terrible," William grumbled as he took a small bite of toast. I sighed loudly as I continued to stare out the conservatory windows. The sun was shining brightly, melting some of the snow that had accumulated outside.

"What?" he asked.

"To me that is a sign that whoever Roza had taught is gone, those secrets dying with them." I smiled weakly. He tried to smile, taking my hand across the table.

"I am sorry, my love." He stroked my fingers softly. "I hope that will be the end of your suffering."

I smiled back at him. I could tell it must have looked strained.

"Whatever Gabriel has done should not cause you suffering, especially since you were so angered by his actions," he continued.

"It is not that. Gabriel even agreed; it is not over. Something does not feel right." I tried to soften my expression. I didn't want him to know how worried I was.

"Can we discuss this later? I would not want it to ruin your day. Let us enjoy our meal." He offered to pour me some more tea.

"Of course, my apologies," I said, taking a sip of my drink. The ratio of tea to blood was too heavy to call it tea any longer. "I only noticed the bread last night at dinner; I am quite alarmed I did not catch it sooner."

"You have had many other things on your mind. It is not surprising."

I hesitated, and then asked him, "Why does it distress me so?"

"Perhaps you hide something more serious."

"When did you get so wise?"

"I love you, Katrine. With love comes some understanding."

I took his hand and gently kissed his knuckles. "And I love you, William."

"I wonder if moving Gabriel to the underground would help you relax."

"I was going to speak further to Charles...."

He lifted his hand. "No need, I already did. He agrees it would be best."

"You...you spoke for me?"

"No, sweetheart. I merely made a suggestion. I know how you hate the idea of someone speaking on your behalf."

"Come now, William, you know it's not meant to be negative towards you. I trust your judgment, and I am pleased that Charles has been spoken with, regardless." I explained, smiling widely at him. "It is something I must get used to, because you do not have the same motherly intent as others who have spoken for me have. My mother never taught me the finer points of having a husband, and she was quite a defiant wife. Perhaps she was not the best example to learn from."

He patted my hand. "I would not change who you are for anything. I am so pleased we had this time together, for today is a busy day for both of us. With everything going on a busy day such as this may turn to a busy several days. Vincenzo and I have some major trading deals going on."

"I am aware. I wish I could come along, but Gigi has other plans." I finished my drink and the last piece of cheese on my plate. "Which reminds me, I don't mean to rush but I would prefer if Gigi did not interrupt us. I am sorry."

"Of course," he said. He stood with me and waited as I smoothed my skirt, adjusting my plain white dress.

William quickly took me in his arms and kissed me full on the lips, my body immediately reacted and I melted into his arms. My lips moved with his as our kiss deepened, passion rising like heat between us.

I wanted to touch his bare skin, feel the warmth of his body against my own as we were locked in an embrace. I wanted to give myself over to him completely, his hand slipping down to my waist only causing more emotions to rise inside me. But I knew I could not so easily, there were too many factors at stake to take such risks.

He was my intended, so it would come eventually.

I pulled away from him, my eyes still closed as I caught my breath.

"My body shall leave but my heart always remains," William whispered in my ear, quickly walking away before I could say a word. I watched him; his strong back and the square of his shoulders; the line of his hair at the base of his neck; until he was out of sight. Hannah quickly came around the corner, signalling me that it was time for me to get ready to leave.

Gigi's eyes narrowed as she watched me from the edge of the stage. I tried to correct whatever I was doing improperly before she said anything, we had been rehearsing for hours and her frustration was getting more aggressive every time she spoke.

"Katrine, what are you doing?" she asked.

I exhaled loudly and sat down in the middle of the stage. "I do not know but I am sure you will tell me."

"What you were doing was quite lovely then you switched to something different, why?" It was the first nice thing I had heard from Gigi while on stage in days.

"You were staring at me like I needed to be corrected, so I thought I would save you the trouble," I replied.

She watched me in silence for a few moments, and then said, "Perhaps you should go to the underground for a longer break and some refreshment."

I stood and left without another word. I had no energy to argue with her at that moment.

I descended the stairs backstage and stepped out into the underground; there was quite a commotion coming from another of the stairwells, people were leaving their rooms to see what all the fuss was about.

Vincenzo appeared first, scanning the crowd then rushing forward when his eyes landed on me.

"Oh! Katrine! I did not know you were here. Perhaps we should go...," he began, trying to pull me back to the stairwell.

"I cannot. Gigi will explode if I go back up now. Why? What's going on?" I asked. Then I heard the shackles dragging across the floor, feet struggling to pull the heavy chains along.

"Is it really necessary to put him in chains? He is not going to run anywhere, you know that!" I exclaimed. I tried to push past to get to Gabriel. All I had wanted was for him to stop bothering the maids.

"This is not what I wanted!" I said sharply. Vincenzo grabbed my shoulders and held me firmly in place; I was surprised at how strongly his fingertips pushed into me.

"You will stay where you are. You will not move or say a word, do you understand me?" The force of his voice made me pause.

"But Gabriel...," I said quietly, and then I heard a giggle. I stared into his green eyes in disbelief as the scraping metal got closer, the stench of dirt and filth coming into the room first like it was its own person. It was almost as surprising as the person who came in, dragging the shackles that were secured to her ankles, her stringy orange hair lying matted in long strands down her face.

She still smiled at me, unashamed of her dirty teeth and dishevelled appearance. Her eyes sparkled in defiance when we made eye contact.

"Pleased to see me, little rat?" Klara Von Dores asked proudly. The foul stench of her breath could clear the room.

I was speechless as she walked past me, flanked by Charles and one of the other male shifters, Mathilde and William bringing up the rear.

Mathilde came over and touched her hand to my cheek, saying quietly, "Vous êtes en sécurité," then she continued on after them.

William only smiled, his expression trying to show me that he did not know ahead of time, and not to blame him for this situation.

I knew in my heart I was safe, but the idea that the dead could suddenly reappear was very distressing.

"What does this mean?" I asked Vincenzo quietly.

"She is a fugitive now. She will have to stand trial before her fate is decided." He did not try to lower his voice as he explained. "Apparently she killed her captor and has been slaughtering her way home from the Holy Land."

"So why is she not in Vienna?"

He frowned. "Apparently whoever captured her thought it best to bring her here. As to why, I am sure Charles would be more equipped to explain."

Klara turned her head to smile and wink at me as she continued down the hallway.

"Gabriel *must* stay at the chateau." I immediately started to panic. "I will not have him anywhere *near* her! I don't care how annoying he has become!"

"William told Charles as much. It is a risk not worth taking. Apparently Charles has a plan for him, so you do not need to worry. Charles is quite concerned that he will have to face your wrath with Klara's reappearance." Vincenzo kept his hand on my shoulder as he spoke in an attempt to keep me calm.

"I am sure he has a good reason, and I am quite curious to hear it. This will be a fantastic story," I said. Vincenzo loosened his grip and we followed along after the group.

William slowed down so he could walk with us.

"I didn't know," he confessed to me.

"*We* didn't know," Vincenzo added.

I smiled at them both. "I know that. You make me seem like a dragon lady."

"No, my love. We just know you don't like things hidden from you, and I am sure Charles would have told you but I get the impression this all happened rather quickly." William's fingertips gently brushed my hand where it hung by my side. "So the plans for Gabriel have to be changed."

Mathilde snorted when she heard my cousin's name. Perhaps she was more pleased to have the potential danger than the former flame down here with her.

"I apologise, Mathilde." Her shifter hearing made so I could speak quietly. "I was only thinking about the irritation at the chateau. I promise you will be consulted."

She turned her head and smiled, winking. "Merci, petite."

Klara sighed as she stepped inside her cell. "Ahhh! It's so nice to be home!"

"I am so pleased you find this amusing. You have caused us all a great deal of trouble! Do you have any idea what is coming?" Charles stalked angrily outside the cell.

"What is that, Lord Westwick? I shall be judged by a jury of my peers? The Old Ones will decide I should be executed?" Klara began, her voice heavy with contempt. "Why do you think I was trying to get to Vienna? My parents want me gone. Do you not think it appropriate they take me from this earth? I did not kill anyone who did not deserve it."

"Who are you to decide something of that magnitude?" Charles snapped.

"Who are my supposed peers?" She cackled loudly. "A courtesan? An impoverished noble? A runaway sorcerer who hides his past? Or, best of all, the farm girl turned lady? Granddaughter of the Beast of Csejthe?"

William and Vincenzo grabbed me before I could move. I was tired of this girl. I was sure I had been tired of her since the first time I'd seen her.

"Best of all, The Old Ones converge on Paris and decide its best to erase me from the earth and take turns tearing me apart! It's ludicrous! You should just kill me now and save them the trouble." Klara's proclamations were so loud I am sure they could be heard from the street.

Charles paused, and then said very calmly. "I should have killed you rather than sent you away, saving my poor friends life. But his death will not be in vain. You will suffer for your crimes. I will do everything in my power to make sure of that."

"Your power?" Klara scoffed at him. William shot a spark at her, causing her to stumble. He continued to use his magic to close and lock the cell, remove her shackles, bring them out and place them on the ground.

I smiled proudly. He had been practicing.

"Power is not something that needs to be discussed. You are not the only one who can be ruthless." Charles stood tall in front of the cell like I imagined a great commander would. He smiled; the look gave me a cold chill.

"So enjoy your time alone, Klara," I chimed in, my voice forceful and sharp. "I hope you spend that time worrying about exactly what is going to happen to you because, and you can trust me when I say this, you won't see it coming and it will be the stuff nightmares are made of."

We all turned and walked out of the room.

Klara's voice called out before the door closed. "I bet you are enjoying this, aren't you, little rat?"

I turned back and smiled proudly at her. "Every single moment."

ARRIVAL

Gabriel came into the salon with Charles the next night, keeping his distance from me. It appeared as if nothing had happened and he was back in Charles's good graces. I was sure he had a totally relevant explanation and I could not wait to hear it.

A large cloaked figure stood in the shadows, quietly drinking and eating a small plate of food. I could not help but watch, my curiosity leaving all thoughts of proper decorum behind.

"Who, or what, is that?" I asked Gigi, gesturing towards the figure.

"That is a bounty hunter, petite. It is customary to extend them some hospitality when they complete their work," she explained, glancing briefly at the figure.

"Why can we not see its face?"

"Because that would defeat its purpose. You can't run if you know what they look like."

"And what of the Old Ones?"

She turned to me and said sharply, "Do not worry about them until we know for sure they are coming. That âne does not garner such attention."

Mathilde sighed loudly as she watched Gabriel walk the room with Charles. She had taken to sitting with Gigi and I in the salon; she looked like a lost child as she sat to my right on a stool with her hands folded in her lap, her red skirts pooling around her feet.

"I am sure he is sorry." I spoke quietly to her. She turned her head so I could see her profile, her blonde curls swaying as she moved.

"I am sure he is," she answered, "but that does not change anything."

William walked in the room with Vincenzo, and as I looked at him I understood, strangely, what she must be going through. How one feels cannot erase betrayal. I remembered how horrible I had felt when William had gone to the brothel, or when he was so angry when I had disobeyed him and killed the slave master who had purchased Gabriel, then would not tell him the absolute truth.

But I had forgiven him.

We had forgiven each other.

"Could you not find a way to forgive him?" I asked her.

She smiled again. "I can try, but I do not have much capacity for forgiveness."

Charles sat Gabriel on a chair a little ways from us then came over to greet us.

"Tis a fine evening, don't you agree, ladies?" Charles greeted us happily, grinning ear to ear. "Might I add, you all look ravishing. Dancing has done lovely things to your figure, Katrine."

"Flattery will not aid your cause, my Lord." I looked away from him quickly to try to hide my blush. I had grown stronger and had muscles I did not know existed. I was pleased all my hard work had not gone unnoticed.

"Katrine, please! I can assure you I only have your best interests at heart. Gabriel is on a strict probation and is monitored quite closely, and you will be able to watch Klara die with your own eyes this time. I thought you would be pleased." His tone and expression made it seem that he was being genuine.

"I have seen too much death in my young life already. But I will be pleased to know she is really gone," I said, looking up at him. "I trust your judgment, Charles."

"Thank you. I trust that the new show is ready to open, Gigi?"

he asked.

"It will be our best yet," she snapped. She was about to continue when her eyes moved to a new guest who had just entered. A tall, pale woman with dark hair peppered with silver cast an imposing glance around the room before coming towards us. She wore a high cut gown of dark brown satin.

"Sainte Mére de Dieu," Gigi cursed. "Charles, what did that girl do?"

When Charles's eyes caught sight of the woman he did not seem surprised but he did appear a little frightened.

"Lord Westwick?" The woman had a blank expression, as if she knew quite well who he was but was just being polite. I felt William's hand on the back of my chair and Vincenzo stood beside Gigi.

"Yes. May I help you?" Charles asked.

She handed him a small letter sealed with black wax. "I am here to discuss certain matters on behalf of Les Vieux. Do you have a moment?"

Charles nodded, extending his arm to the woman as they walked away. She did not take it, but walked directly beside him. We sat in shocked silence for several moments.

"What did she do?" Gigi asked Vincenzo in Italian. They spoke in certain languages when they only wanted certain people to understand.

"We did not receive the full account," Vincenzo told her in his native language.

"But we do know that the man Charles sent her with was slaughtered, along with his family, and his house burnt to the ground," Mathilde explained, the conversation continuing on in the same language. "Small children and animals as well. Anything that happened to be on the property."

"She claims the man violated her," William added. I had questions, but since my speaking Italian was poor I decided just to listen.

"She was picked up on the Austrian border with another woman. A vampire with no tongue. This happened after several incidents where Klara was, well, Klara. She and this girl slaughtered a whole tavern in Monaco. We don't know how they got there; we don't know where they had been. We don't know fully what she has done, but we know a lot of people are angry." Vincenzo eyes lowered as he pondered, "I have heard the legend of the vampire with no tongue. I am surprised she would fraternise with the likes of Klara."

Gigi huffed loudly. "What a mess that girl has created! The poor Baron must be beside himself."

"Who do you think hired the bounty hunter?" Mathilde chuckled.

"So since we took her on we must make sure her execution is carried out? I wonder if Charles thinks his little trip was worth all of this trouble." Gigi could not hide the glimmer in her eye as she speculated at Charles's mistake.

As if on cue Natalia came in with Sybilla, Morgana was not far behind. The last two came immediately to us, while Natalia searched the room for Charles.

"Did you know?" I asked Morgana quietly when she took her seat directly beside me. Mathilde pulled her stool over so we were almost in a semi circle.

"Not directly. But you really do not need to worry about her." Morgana leaned in to me, smoothing the skirt of her plain grey dress.

"Is there something I need to worry about?"

"Not clearly," she held out her hand and I touched mine to hers. I got a quick flash of a dark haired woman, looking panicked and scared. She seemed oddly familiar.

"It appears you get to keep some of those powers you absorbed." Morgana smiled. "As you have just seen I have nothing clear yet. But I am overwhelmed by the idea that your mother is alive."

I took a deep breath in and out. "One thing at a time. What about Klara?"

"She has done something truly horrific things," she said, pulling her hand away from mine. "Death will be a kind of punishment for her crimes."

Sybilla smiled at me as she sat quietly beside Gigi. My friend had truly blossomed under Gigi's influence; she was the picture of grace and an absolutely stunning beauty. Smiling and nodding my approval, I was glad she was with us.

The woman with Charles paused when she saw Sybilla. She examined the girl in a way that made me shiver and suddenly very protective.

Sybilla did not notice, calmly smoothing her green skirt so it lay perfectly flat while she sat and listening to our conversations.

The woman said something to Charles, it appeared to be about Sybilla, I could tell by his expression it was something quite troubling.

"Do not forget that we know very little about her. But I do not believe her to be a threat, I would have seen something if it was otherwise," Morgana's voice was like a voice in my own head. I sighed, smoothing a piece of hair around my face.

Vincenzo and Gigi continued speaking in Italian. William stood tense at my back and Mathilde watched Gabriel as he sat quietly in the same chair Charles had put him in. He actually seemed quite content to simply sit and watch the comings and goings of the other people. He had been in seclusion since we'd left Russia almost eleven months before.

Thinking of the time that had passed my heart began to ache. It had almost been a year since my Grandmother had died.

It seemed like it was just yesterday.

"My, how time flies," I said out to no one in particular. It also meant that Mathilde may not have even seen him in all this time.

Gabriel turned and smiled at me, the first time he had looked directly at me all evening.

No matter what he had done, he was still my family. And we had survived. I smiled back.

The next day Sybilla and I rode together to rehearsal. She looked as if she had not slept.

"Something troubling you, mon ami?" I asked. We were alone, which seemed to put her at ease. Gigi had left much earlier to speak with Josephine about the costumes.

"I am quite nervous about several things." She looked as if she had spent quite a lot of time thinking about her troubles. "I am concerned about the show. I have not had such a key role and I am worried I cannot pull it off. I am also worried about these 'old ones'."

"Whatever for? They are not here for you."

"No, but I believe I have encountered them before and for some reason I do not remember. That frightens me. But that is not my only memory gap."

"You are safe with us, Sybilla. It is only natural to be concerned about the show, but I can assure you it will pass with time." I pat her knee and tried to be reassuring.

"I would not want to disappoint Grisela," she said.

I rolled my eyes. "Yes, because your greatest concern in this world should be not disappointing Grisela."

"Are you not concerned about that?" she asked.

"Of course I am but not to the same degree. As long as you try your best she will be happy."

She smiled, but she appeared unsure. "I do hope so."

We finally arrived at the theatre, stepping out into the stifling heat. Cold nights and increasingly hot days were making Paris quite smelly and almost unbearable.

I covered my nose and mouth and started up the stairs. Something flashed in the corner of my eye; I turned to see just the profile of a brown haired woman before she disappeared into the crowd.

I watched for a few minutes, just in case I noticed something significant or familiar. But she simply disappeared; I could not even see any sign of her passing through the crowd.

This situation seemed strangely familiar.

"Katrine? Katrine, are you coming?" Sybilla called out to me. I turned and continued on, there was no point in stopping and dwelling on the past.

Gigi did not notice us as we approached the stage; she was too involved in directing the others. She had been pushing one girl, I believed her name was Rosalie, extra hard. The girl was becoming quite an accomplished dancer. Gigi believed the extra push could bring her to greatness.

"So pleased you two could join us," Gigi said without turning her head. "Take your places please."

We exchanged a quick glance before quietly moving into our places. I lifted the edge of my skirt until it was slightly above my ankles and when the cane slammed into the stage and the rhythm began I started to dance.

The pounding flowed through me and I fell in sync as if it was my own heartbeat. My feet glided with ease across the stage and I wished for less constrictive clothing. I wanted to move and spin as if I was flowing in the wind. I felt such ease and peace that I lost track of the real world and everyone in it.

I only wanted to be present in that moment, where nothing else mattered except the dance. There were no threats, pressures, no pains. No people bent on destruction, only the freedom and joy of movement and where all of it would carry you.

One of the men stumbled and the dance halted. I waited quietly as he righted himself; his closeness to Rosalie made it an issue. He was a shifter, his gruff appearance caused him to resemble a farm hand but he was quite light on his feet. He spoke accented French and I believed he, like Charles, was from England.

He was quite a contrast to the petite Rosalie; with flowing dark hair and pale skin she looked as if she was plucked from a painting. Her small build made her appear childlike, and when she held out her hand to the man his hand totally engulfed hers like it swallowed it whole.

This time when we began again I watched them; they touched and moved with each other, locked eyes with such fire in their gaze they seemed as if they were lovers.

Something inside me reacted and I suddenly wanted William. I wanted to experience what they were feeling. Watching them made me think that dancing was as close as one could get to true passion with another person without actually making love.

Sybilla seemed to notice it as well, her eyes mixed with admiration and envy. I could not help but wonder if she had ever loved someone in such a manner.

Gigi worked us hard for she would have nothing less than perfection. She seemed happiest when she had something to control, and she arranged a show with a grace and extravagance that Charles never seemed to have.

The only trouble was that now she seemed to do very little dancing herself.

As Gigi watched Rosalie and her partner dance I saw a spark of something, only for a brief second. I remembered that Vincenzo had said once that Gigi and Charles had had a long affair, but I had heard nothing else about her love life.

I hoped Charles was not the only man she had ever loved. I could not imagine he was capable of loving only one woman at a time.

We continued on for what seemed like hours, then Gigi dismissed us. I sat on the edge of the stage and waited while everyone was cleared.

I saw something in the darkness, movement at the back of the room that was well hidden when the stage lights were bright. I could do nothing but watch, waiting to see if my eyes were playing tricks or we had a visitor.

I heard Sybilla and Gigi behind me, and I could tell by the topic of conversation that we were alone.

"Which of your parents is a vampire, child?" Gigi asked Sybilla.

"I do not know. Both the parents I know are human. My mother only told me briefly of the vampire prince who was really my father, though the father I know was a Turkish prince." Sybilla's expression lightened when she spoke of her parents. "I am wondering if this vampire prince is one of The Old Ones. Do you know them well? Is it at all possible?"

Gigi hesitated before saying, "I do not know off hand but I shall look into it."

Sybilla said thank you then took her leave, smiling at me as she walked out of the theatre.

I stood and met Gigi's troubled expression, her eyebrows lowered as she stared into the darkness.

"What is the trouble?" I asked.

"If I am correct, I cannot tell her what I know." Gigi's looked troubled. "It will break her heart."

I stood and righted myself, smoothing the front of my skirts.

"You know it has almost been a year, petite. Do you think you shall ever wear colour again?" Gigi asked as we began to head out of the theatre. The warm weather had come, and I knew that would happen eventually but I did not think it would be so soon.

"I had not thought about it, I thought I had more time," I said.

"That is the thing about time, it goes on whether you like it or not," Gigi replied, taking my arm as we stepped out into the street. "We shall enjoy the summer in Paris, which I am sure will lighten your spirits."

"A public execution will not lighten my spirits."

Gigi smiled. "You may be pleasantly surprised."

SERIOUS CONVERSATION

Vincenzo occasionally looked over at me as he sat writing letters. He had two stacks beside his writing space; one side with blank pages the other with folded and sealed pages ready to post.

"Do you have to watch me so closely?" he asked without looking up from his work.

"I do not get to see you much." I perched on a stool beside his table. "If that is what I need to do to spend time with you then so be it. And Gabriel spent lots of time watching me at my toilette."

"Are you trying to fill that void by doing the same with me?"

My eyebrows furrowed. "No. I am sure he and I could return to that state if I sincerely wished to do so."

"Well, I must tell you that it would probably be very entertaining to watch him now, with the work that Charles has him doing."

"I am here to spend time with you, mon ami. What is wrong with that?" I said, pausing before I asked, "What is he doing, anyhow?"

Vincenzo smiled to himself. "Kitchen duties. Frankly I think it looks good on him. He has probably never had to do hard labour a day in his life."

"And you have?"

He chuckled. "One day I will tell you of my life before I came to be here. I am sure you will be surprised, if not shocked."

"Once you said to me that the one who turned you gave you powers," I said.

"Yes, the one who turned me made me so much more than a simple vampire." He hesitated, and then continued, "Perhaps when you are open to the idea of speaking of sexual relations I can explain it to you, because it's tied into it."

My stomach jumped into my throat when he mentioned sex. I had always thought of it as something that was only done by a married couple, to create babies. Beyond that it had never come up.

"Perhaps it is something I should think about," I replied, "if I am to become William's wife."

He stopped and turned to me. "Do you still believe you should only have sex with your husband?"

I stared blankly at him and he laughed. "I am not saying you can whore yourself around but things are not as they were, you do not have to follow common rules anymore. If you wish to engage in such matters without marriage it is acceptable, within reason of course."

"To be completely honest I had not put much thought into it, but I guess I should," I said. "The world is a different place. Perhaps William will expect it."

"If he does he is not the man I thought he was, and not worth such a gift."

"So what does that have to do with you and your condition?"

He turned back to his work. "Along with craving blood I also crave sex, and feed on sexual energy. A term I once heard for the condition is incubus, but I don't speak of it much because it frightens people."

"When you kissed me in Russia, did you..."

"That was part of it, yes. I'm sorry Katrine. I hope you do not feel violated."

I smiled, even though he wasn't looking. "No, I do not. Is that why you do not have a female companion? Why none of the other women..."

"That would be a question for them, mon ami."

"So unless you....and even with blood, you are never completely satisfied?"

He paused. "I have spent many years with this affliction, Katrine. I have found ways to sate myself."

I smiled again and nodded while he went back to his work.

"That is quite a bit of correspondence for one day," I said after several minutes of silence.

"It comes with the business," he told me. "When you are in the business of buying and selling things on occasion you have to find something, and in some instances it is not an easily accessible item or they would get it themselves."

"Anything interesting?"

"Another alchemist who needs something strange and unusual." He flipped through his pages. "This happening to be saffron from a particular region in India."

"Shall we have to go collect it ourselves?" I asked happily.

"Non, mon ami. I don't think there will be any trips until after the execution," he said.

"How exactly will that go about? Will she hang or burn?"

He laughed. "My dear, sweet child. If tradition is followed she will be decapitated, her heart cut out and burned, and the ashes thrown in a river running in two different directions."

I started blankly at him, completely speechless. I could not fully comprehend the idea of that, the brutality like nothing I had ever heard of.

"Is that the way it is always done?" I finally asked him after a long pause, my voice unsteady.

"Unfortunately, yes." He had little emotion as he explained further. "It seems to be the only thing that is totally effective. Perhaps that is why Klara still stands after all that has happened. I also must add that I sincerely hope you will only have to witness one of these sorts of executions."

"I think it is the reality of the world we live in, like the view of women as property," I replied.

"All you may do is hope one day things will change. Maybe, with time, another form of vampire execution will be found. It took some time to find that one."

I stood and smoothed my skirt. "While I rather enjoy our conversations, I believe I should take my leave now before Gigi comes looking."

"Is she well?" he asked.

"To the best of my knowledge. Why? Do you know something I don't?"

"No. Sometimes I am not a good friend to her, and I would like to try to change that."

"Of course. I will inform you if there is a change," I said, and I took my leave.

What he had said had piqued my interest, so I went to the kitchen.

Gabriel was standing at the counter wearing an old brown apron, looking quite pleased with himself as he peeled and chopped vegetables.

He smiled proudly when he saw me. "Isn't it marvellous, cousin? I am finding such joy in the simplest tasks. Perhaps I shall become a cook!"

His enthusiasm was infectious and I could not help but smile, by the looks of the servants his enthusiasm was rapidly spreading.

"I am pleased you are enjoying yourself, but this is supposed to be a punishment," I said.

"I see it as more of a learning experience. Reminding me of how the world really is, keeping me humble and grounded in this life." He gazed proudly at his work. "I realised that I was living too much in the past and holding on to old beliefs. But I am not that man anymore and I must adapt or die."

"I am so pleased you have found some enlightenment."

"How have you adapted so well?

"I was not long in my other life, cousin; I had very little to hold on to. I was at an age where things would greatly change because I would have to marry."

"Yes, women have so many more life changes then men do," he said. "But regardless of any of that, this is something I need to work on. The past must remain where it is."

"Then I shall leave you to it," I replied. I turned and left without another word.

As I approached the main entryway I heard voices, and was surprised to see that the representative for The Old Ones had returned.

I merged into the back of the receiving line and listened quietly to what was going on.

Natalia stood beside Charles as if she was his wife; she looked quite proud but also a bit frightened when you looked her in the eyes. She wore a pretty green dress trimmed with lace that looked new.

"I am honoured that you have returned but I did not know you were coming so we are not equipped to receive you." Charles hid his discomfort well. I was getting to know him better so I could see he was not pleased by this unannounced arrival. Gigi joined the group and stood close beside me, her expression souring when she saw Natalia.

"No need, Lord Westwick. I have only come to notify you that Les Vieux has passed their judgment." She handed Charles a sealed letter. "Prepare your people and this theatre of yours; we believe it is the only place suitable for such an event."

I felt Gigi's body tense; the idea of blood spilling in such a fashion on our stage was unsettling.

Charles said nothing for a few moments and we all stood in silence.

Finally, he said, "Of course, but some time shall be needed to prepare. I shall notify you when I am able."

"Do not take too long, Lord Westwick," she told him sharply. "We shall not wait for long. Then passing the sentence would become your responsibility."

She left so quickly we barely had time to bow. Charles turned and went straight upstairs, returning to his study to read the message and consider the situation.

Gigi began to curse rapidly and I followed her to our rooms.

"The theatre! The theatre! Can you imagine petite?" Gigi started after slamming the door to her room closed. "If he even suggests that we do it...."

"Why would he sully our stage in such a manner?" I asked.

Gigi scoffed at me with a condescending glance. "Do you not know by now that Charles is not very bright? He would move the heavens to make himself look good in the eyes of those he believes are superior."

"Even to jeopardise his business?"

"He is not thinking of that, ma petite, and that is what makes him stupid. Did you see how he paraded that poor young woman around like a prized pig? Can you imagine how he would behave if they brought a child into this world?"

"A child?"

"Yes, he has found his famed mythological creature. You don't think he will do everything he can to tie himself to her?"

"Do you think he loves her?"

Gigi snickered. "Stop being naive, petite. He is a man, through and through."

"That *is* unfortunate." I could think of nothing else to say. I watched Gigi walk around her room, organising things, something I had watched her do many times. I wanted to ask her about the things Vincenzo said, about sexual relations, but it did not seem like the right time. She sat at her toilette while I sat near the back of the room; she slowly started to remove the pins from her hair. I noticed for the first time as her curls began to fall that she had some streaks of white running through the gold. She looked tired. Today I noticed it around her eyes.

"Something on your mind, petite?" she asked me.

"Nothing specific. Did you see Gabriel in the kitchens?"

"No. But I have been told it was amusing. Now, we need to work on your speaking languages for when we must see The Old Ones. Which are you the least confident speaking?"

"Greek. And my Latin could use some work, but if I need to I can manage."

"And your Italian?" she asked in that language.

I smiled. "Penso che sia fantastico, signora. Sei un insegnante meravigliaso."

Before she could say more, I said in my native tongue, "I am sure it will not be necessary, but I have this language also."

She rolled her eyes. "Don't be smart. Cockiness will give you wrinkles."

THE ONLY ONE

Natalia eyed me as she danced with Charles the following evening in the salon. The new show would open tomorrow and I was attempting to relax, her staring was making me uncomfortable. Gigi and Sybilla, who sat close to me, did not seem to notice. Neither did William, who stood a little ways behind me chatting with Vincenzo.

I could not imagine what she would possibly want with me.

She managed to pull away from Charles and came and sat with the group, something she had not done often. She pulled a chair as close as she could without being on my lap, grinning ear to ear.

"Pardon me, Lady Bathory, but may I speak with you in privacy?" Natalia asked me. She struggled to put the sentence together; she had not taken well to a new spoken language.

"Please call me Katrine," I said. "May I ask what this is about? Because..."

"No, no. Somewhere else." She took my hand, stood and beckoned me to follow. I sighed loudly and we began to walk together around the room.

"Um, I am sorry Katrine. I am embarrassed, but there is very little time for privacy," she started, "and I don't know how to fix problem.

You know Lord Westwick, yes?"

"Yes, but I don't..."

"He is nice man, has treated me very kind and I enjoy his company. But, he wishes to...and I do not want for...what you French call relations sexuelles."

I hesitated. "Oh."

"You must understand, I have no wish to do such things with anyone. I don't know what to tell him. He thinks we should breed. Can you imagine?"

"Natalia, you must tell him the truth."

"But he will send me away! That is why I ask your help. He admires you. Also adores you, and Miss Delphine. You make him understand. Please, I am begging you. I need help! I am afraid!"

I took the girl's arm in mine, pat the top of her hand gently as Gigi had done so many times to me when I was in such a state of panic.

"Such a state will not help anyone, my dear. I fear you would become harder to understand." We continued to walk as I spoke. "But do not fret. I will speak to him, and if I feel ill equipped, with your permission, I will ask Mademoiselle Delphine for assistance."

She squealed in glee and hugged me tightly. I did not have the heart to tell her it may not go as well as she expected.

"Thank you! Thank you! I am in your debt," she said happily, hurrying away from me and back to the group.

I slowly finished my walk and went back to my seat. Luckily Natalia had gone away from my space as not to attract too much attention.

"I assume you will have something to tell me later," Gigi said quietly to me in Latin. Her insistence on me being fluent in as many languages as possible had become such a high priority since the arrival of The Old Ones that she only wanted to converse in the languages I was struggling with.

I attempted to respond in Latin. "It may even bring some light to your sour expression."

She snorted. "I can't imagine. Life does not often grant such small gifts."

"Katrine, I must add something," Natalia's voice was suddenly in my ear, startling me. "It is very important, and I think I missed it before. It is not that I do not wish to have relations with Charles; I do not wish to have relations with anyone. You understand, yes?"

"Yes, of course. And you did tell me, Natalia. I fully understand," I replied.

She nodded and said something in Russian, then turned and walked away.

Gigi said, in flawless Greek, "My word, this must be interesting."

It took several attempts but I was finally able to say, in passable Greek, that she should listen to me more.

"Your Greek is abysmal," she continued on. I rolled my eyes.

William came over to us and held out his hand, asking me to dance.

I stood and went with him and we glided smoothly out on to the dance floor.

We made eye contact and kept our eyes locked as we moved. I did love him, the depth of how much was clear to me when I looked at him.

But I did not know how much of myself I was willing to give to this man, to tie me to him in such a permanent way. I was not the type of girl who would love and embrace many men, I had always believed once I found the right one he would be all I'd ever know, as my parents had.

That was no longer my world, but it did not change how I felt.

Whether or not William was that 'only one' was what I was unsure of.

ANNA

She began picking up the candlesticks, removing the tapers carefully before throwing the heavy piece of wood at him.

"I will deal with your anger over displeasing Les Vieux, Grisela," Charles said sharply. She then proceeded to cross the room to one of the many bookshelves, pulling down the largest volumes within her reach and launching them at him like one would throw a dinner plate.

"Will you do something about this?" Charles snapped at me.

I raised my hands in defeat. "I suggested a room other than the library. There would be fewer things to throw."

He let out an exasperated moan as Gigi continued; it had taken him several days to muster the courage to tell Gigi that her show would have to break for two days to accommodate Klara's execution. He had begun to say it would be postponed but changed his mind when he saw how angry she was.

"Petite, he can speak Latin and Greek. If you must speak with him do it in one of those languages," Gigi told me. I rolled my eyes.

"So you do understand how important this is, Grisela," Charles attempted to speak to her. "It will only be two days, I have already prepared a crew to clean the..."

Gigi paused, pointing at him. "Don't you *dare* say it will be done on the stage!"

"I have no choice. The entire company must be present. It is the only place we can all fit comfortably."

She stared blankly at him for several moments before storming out of the room.

"Please, Katrine. Please try to speak with her," he pleaded with me as I straightened myself to leave.

"I make no promises," I said in terribly broken Greek then followed her out.

"I will not let his foolishness ruin my opening," Gigi said as I closed the door to her room behind us.

"Tonight will be perfect." I tried to sound reassuring. "We will have three full shows before the break, and then we will only miss one because we do not perform on Sundays."

"Are you defending him?"

"No, just trying to make you feel better."

"The blood will be spilled on the same stage you will dance on tonight. Are you fine with that, ma petite?"

"Of course not. But I understand the need to impress," I said in Latin. I smiled, proud that I had spoken the phrase successfully.

She brushed a few of her loose curls away from her face. "You must know that this is one of his dreams for us. He would love nothing more than for the Danse Macabre to become a feature on the world's stage, and for himself to be recognised as a powerful being."

"He told you this?"

Her eyes went glossy with the beginning of tears. "Yes, that is how he got me to join him. I believed whole heartily in his dreams. That was a long time ago."

"Did you love him?"

"Then I did. But that person has been gone for a long time." She pat her eyes with a handkerchief. "But enough of this. We must go to the theatre."

"I saw something," Morgana said as we rode in the bumpy carriage.

"Please Lord tell me it's not Gigi number three." Gigi crossed herself.

"No, this one is for Katrine." Morgana gestured to me. "I must begin by saying it is not entirely clear, the pictures are still a bit fuzzy. But I do see a woman who looks like your mother, and she is angry."

"I am unsure of how to react to that," I told her.

"I will tell you if I see more, but that is all I have seen for some time and I have had that vision on more than one occasion." Morgana tried to look reassuring and failed.

"Please do not take this personally, ma petite, but I am overwhelmed with relief that it's not about me," Gigi added.

"After what happened in Russia, no one would blame you," Morgana said.

"Who else could it be?" I asked. "So we should prepare for an attack, is that what you are saying?"

"I told you, it is not clear. So do what you believe is best." Morgana tried to hide her frustration; she looked like she was getting angry.

"You sound as if you are cross with me, Morgana." I watched her as I asked to see if I could judge if she was truly annoyed.

"I have told you what I can, and it frustrates me that I cannot prepare you."

"That is not your responsibility. All you can do is say something is coming. I must prepare for myself."

"You cannot always be on high alert. You must live your life." Morgana touched my sleeve.

"There are times in your life where you can relax and just live. Now is not one of those times. We must always be aware of our environment," Gigi explained. "I must say that timing in these situations is always terrible."

I caught the full effect of Gigi's outfit when we stepped out of the carriage. She wore a light cloak over her dress that shimmered like the glow of moonlight.

I had no time to compliment her, the crowd outside the theatre was so large Morgana and I had to go from the carriage to the underground without stopping. Since Gigi had been directing the shows our popularity had grown, she was loved as a dancer, and it seemed more so as a creator. I was not surprised we had a packed house for our latest premiere.

The underground was busy but calm, moving like a well oiled machine. Morgana immediately went to her duties as Josephine's assistant; I noticed she had picked up another set of hands.

"Good evening, cousin," I said to Gabriel, who was hunched over hemming a garment. "I am surprised to see you here."

"This was another of Charles's suggestions. I preferred the kitchens, but I am gaining some appreciation for what you all put into these shows," he replied.

"And you are doing a fine job for a former nobleman," Josephine added as she handed me my costume.

"This is quite easy compared to stitching up wounds on a battlefield." Gabriel had a strange smile as he reflected on the situation.

"My apologies, Gabriel. I assumed you had a sheltered life," Josephine said. I went behind the screen and began to put on my costume.

"It is a common misconception that the Eastern Royal Families live the posh life of the royals of Western Europe," Gabriel replied. "There is so much fighting and back stabbing, even among family, that you do not ever feel power without knowing loneliness and fear. I believe that my other life ended because I disagreed with someone more powerful then myself, and I was not strong enough to do anything about it. My own people had me assassinated."

I came out from behind the screen and went to Gabriel, placing a hand on his shoulder. "Let's not speak of that now. This is an important night. I wouldn't want to spoil it."

He smiled and nodded. "Of course. I shall wait for you here afterwards, and then perhaps we can return to the chateau afterwards?"

"That would be lovely," I replied. Josephine came to me and began to tie some of the ribbons on my costume. It was simple and blue with ribbons and French lace, Gigi said it was childlike but I didn't think so.

I had no main part in this production, I was waiting for Gigi to cast me in a lead but she hadn't done it yet. I did not question her taste, but I would like a lead.

I walked up the stairwell towards the stage, the same stairwell I had walked up many times. The same stairwell where Klara's man had attacked me then used to return to the underground where she had tried to kill me. It seemed strange that such a small place would hold so much meaning to me.

I stepped out of the doorway and into the wings. I watched as the others took their places then slowly went to mine. Sybilla stood in her place, looking restless and uneasy. She smiled uncomfortably at me. I smiled back. I wished there was something I could do for her.

But then the curtain dropped and all thoughts left me except my movements as they went in time to the music.

It was all over as quickly as it had begun, and soon we were standing in our places again with the curtain lowered.

The others went to each other and spoke a bit while I went

straight for the stairs and back to the underground.

Gabriel waited patiently for me as I changed and cleaned myself up.

He held out his arm to me and lead me back towards the stairs that would bring us up to the front entry way. I picked up the edge of my snowy white skirt as we went up the stairs.

"You even look beautiful in mourning wear," Gabriel said as we stepped out into the crowded main entry.

"Why don't you wear any?" I asked him. "She was your cousin."

He opened his mouth, closed it again, and then said, "I do not know. I am not worthy."

We crossed the room and headed to the large flight of stairs that would take us to the private boxes.

I felt a presence come closer to us, I couldn't figure out who or what it was. Gabriel seemed to feel it too because he turned around to meet it face to face.

"It can't be," he said quietly.

"They said you were here." Gabriel's face went as white as a sheet as a female voice spoke. "They said you had become one of the others but I didn't believe them. I said Gabor Bathory would never do such a thing, he is an honourable man..."

I turned and the woman gasped when she saw my face. I tried to hold back my shock, as if I wasn't looking into the face of a young Countess Erzsebet Bathory but with a sharper nose.

It was my mother's face in many ways, but angry, just like Morgana had said.

"So she does exist!" The woman gestured angrily at me. "And she wears mourning clothes for her! How fitting! Have you known all along about this Gabor? Did you know about her mother also?"

"Anna, please, you don't understand. It's not that simple."

"Do you not wish to know who I am, girl?" the woman snapped.

I stood and stared at her, too frightened to say anything at all.

She grabbed my right hand and pulled roughly so she could see my ring. She tried to pull it off my hand but my reflexes were too quick and she stumbled as I hugged my hand to my chest.

"You are Anna Bathory, my grandmother's oldest...," I managed to sputter out.

"My name is Anna Nadasdy." She corrected me, her tone full of anger. "My husband's name made me Anna Zrinyi. You may address me as Countess Zrinyi! But do not get confused, I am my father's daughter."

"I know all about my mother's sins, your mother's birth was wrong and you are disgusting! I will never share a name with *you*," she continued. "If it wasn't for the Order I would kill you right now."

"Anna, leave the girl alone," Gabriel said. "It is not her fault. She is just as much a victim as you."

Countess Zrinyi began to laugh. "Are you serious?"

"If you want to blame someone blame Erzsebet!" Gabriel closed some of the distance between them. "But she was one of the only people in this world who showed this girl some kindness and I will not have you make her sound like some kind of demon!"

"I have spent my life in that woman's shadow, it seems only fitting." Countess Zrinyi spoke so dismissively and with such derision I was taken aback.

"What happened to you, Anna?" Gabriel asked, reaching out to her while keeping a tight grip on my arm.

She flinched, taking a small step back. "You should know by now, Gabor. Bathory don't *just die*. Our blood won't allow it. I was ill, and then someone came to me and said I could live again if I gave up my life as I knew it. I was more than happy to be free."

"You said I was too honourable to do such a thing when you did exactly what I did," Gabriel replied.

"But you were a prince! You had a good life! I was surrounded by monsters. I could not bring babies into such a world, and you know that's all I wanted."

"What about Pal? And Kata?"

"Red cares for the young Count, he will be fine. My poor sister is too much like our mother. I can do nothing to save her."

"So you are a blood drinker?" I blurted out.

She smiled, and the look frightened me. "Yes, I suppose I am. The Order has taken very good care of me. I am supposed to tell you, girl, Beatrix Delphine sends her regards."

"My name is..."

"I don't care to know your name!" She exclaimed loud enough I thought I heard an echo. "You should not exist! Gabor, come with me now, back to the Order. You belong with us."

"No," he said flatly.

"What?" she stuttered, completely shocked.

"I will not go with you. I do not belong with the Order," he said with a force I had never heard from him before. I assumed it was the voice of the man who commanded soldiers.

"Why? Because you think they can provide for you? Bathory men have been loyal to the Order for centuries," she replied.

"Now you speak to me of Bathory, only claiming the lineage when it suits you! *How dare you!* Who are you to speak of honour and loyalty when you deny who you are?" He spoke with so much anger and force I thought we would attract attention. "These people and *this girl*, who you are so disgusted by, have shown me more loyalty and kindness than anyone else in my life! She is a Bathory through and through whether you deny her or not!"

"Countess Zrinyi?" I finally had the courage to say. She turned her dark eyes to me and so many reactions went through my mind I was momentarily speechless.

"If you would not mind, could you please deliver a message to Beatrix Delphine for me?" I asked, and she smiled as if she knew some devious secret. Her eyes glanced quickly to the top of the staircase; I wondered if she saw Gigi and believed it to be Beatrix.

"Please tell her 'Then shalt thou walk in thy way safely, and thy foot shall not stumble. When thou liest down, thou shalt not be afraid; yea, thou shalt lie down, and thy sleep shall be sweet'," I said, and the two stared at me with confused expressions.

"I shall tell her. Then perhaps she and I will come and kill you." Countess Zrinyi peered off, smiling oddly to herself. "And your mother. You can watch her die before we deal with you."

Gabriel let go of me and grabbed her forearm, she was trying not to cry out in pain. I felt the presence of several people as they came down the stairs behind me; William, Vincenzo and Gigi stood just steps behind us, and I sensed Morgana move closer to us from within the crowd.

"There will be no more deaths," he said, his voice quiet but full of fire and anger. "You wish for that life, Anna, go have it. I am happy where I am."

She pulled out of his grasp, turning her eyes to me again. "You may call yourself whatever you like, wear her ring, speak her name as if it were gospel. You can even have Gabor's protection. But it is wrong, and you are the child of a bastard! You will always be nothing more than an addition to an indiscretion. You're sick!"

I did the only thing I could think of doing. I smiled my best, most courteous smile at her, remembering all that Gigi had taught me.

"It was a pleasure to finally meet you, Countess Zrinyi," I said with a big grin. "Please do not forget my message to Beatrix Delphine, and in case she is confused please tell her it's from Katrine, but I am sure she won't be."

"When the time comes, Gabor, you will remember your place. Then we shall speak again," Countess Zrinyi said, she stood up straight and brushed back loose strands of her dark hair. As I looked at her face, a mix of my mother and my Grandmother, I couldn't help but think about how beautiful she was. Just like them, the only difference being that nose, which I assumed belonged to The Black Bey.

"I understand why you would admire him," I blurted out as she began to walk away. "If my father was a hero I would want to be connected with him too."

She paused, looked as if she would say something more, then turned and disappeared into the crowd.

Gabriel and I watched in silence as she disappeared into the crowd. Once she was out of sight we went upstairs.

"A friend of yours, petite?" Gigi asked when we got to the top of the staircase.

"Countess Anna Zrinyi, Erzsebet Bathory's oldest daughter," I replied in Latin. "Apparently a new friend of Beatrix's."

Gigi was about to say something until I said, "Do not be concerned. I handled the situation."

"By reciting a bible quote? I do not understand." Gabriel was still hanging on to my arm.

Gigi watched me, and then said with a smirk on her face, "Bon spectacle, ma petite colombe."

I smiled and curtsied. "I was only acting as your representative."

Gabriel let go of my arm, his expression gone blank and his eyes empty and distant.

"Cousin?" I said quietly to him.

"They have Anna," he said flatly. "Why do they have Anna? She is of no use to them."

"I am so sorry, Cousin."

"It is something about our family. But why would they not take Erzsebet?"

"Perhaps they did and we are unaware," I replied, "or she refused."

"If she is the key, why not take her?" he mumbled to himself as he walked away from us towards the boxes.

"Are you alright?" William asked, rushing to my side.

"I am." I took his hand and smiled at him. His brow was

furrowed as if he did not believe me and he was about to accuse me of lying.

"Who was she?" Morgana asked as she came up behind me.

"My Grandmother's oldest legitimate child," I replied.

"She will kill you if given the opportunity." Morgana made the statement in a similar way that one would comment about the weather.

"I figured as much." I sighed loudly, the entire conversation making me exhausted. "Anything else I should know?"

"One day she may grow to accept you, as long as you do not present yourself under false pretences," she proclaimed. She continued on in the direction Gabriel had gone, Vincenzo close behind.

William pulled me closer to him, as if in some way it would help protect me. We stood and watched as Gigi and Charles descended the stairs to a thunderous applause. I had a brief flash in my mind of the two doing something similar but at a different place that glittered and sparkled as if full of crystals.

Gigi turned to Charles and I saw something, only for a brief moment, pass between the two of them. I was unsure what it was; perhaps it was all a glimpse of what might have been, or of the past.

"Shall we return home, my love?" William asked, his hot breath on my neck causing me to shutter.

"That would be wonderful," I replied, allowing him to lead me back down the stairs.

INTRUSIVE

"What are you thinking?"

I stared out at the garden with its buds beginning to flourish into brilliant blooms.

"Morgana said she would kill you." William stated.

"She also said she may accept me," I replied.

"And you trust her?" he asked.

"I have no reason not to." I turned my eyes to him. "She is my Aunt, William. I have never had an aunt before. She is clearly important to Gabriel. It is what my grandmother would have wanted."

"What if Morgana is wrong?"

"William, I have no intention of not protecting myself or all of us if need be. I will just not do anything against her under my own steam," I replied.

"Even if she is involved with Gigi's sister?"

"We will cross that bridge if we come to it. Now, come walk the grounds with me." I grabbed his hand and pulled him off down one of the paths.

"May I ask you something? It is a bit of a sensitive subject," I began as we moved farther away from the house.

"Of course," he said, and before he could say more I continued.

"Have you ever...had relations with a woman?" I asked. "Because I have never, and I didn't know if you were thinking about it."

"About you having had relations with other men?"

"No. About us. Having relations, I mean."

He paused for a moment before saying, "I am unsure of the proper way to respond. I wouldn't want you to think poorly of me. May I think about this before I answer you?"

"Of course," I said, a bit startled by his response. "I guess I had assumed that as a man it was something you spent a considerable amount of time thinking about."

He chuckled. "I suppose it is so with most men but not with me."

"Thank you for telling me."

We walked for a while in silence before we both abruptly stopped, turning to speak.

"You first," I said.

"No, ladies first."

"Did you know...or, perhaps I mean to say did you know of Vincenzo's... carnal appetites?"

He nodded and smiled to himself. "Now I understand."

"What?"

"He finally told you about his need for sexual energy, perhaps by inquiring about your thoughts on the subject, and now it is in your thoughts."

"It would have come up eventually, William."

"Of course, it is only an explanation for your sudden interest." His expression changed, and he began to look sad.

I pulled him to me and whispered, being sure that my breath touched his ear. "Do you think I do not desire you, my love? But a lady must control her urges as not to sully her reputation."

He touched the back of my neck with the tips of his fingers, gently, as if he was using a feather. He kissed my shoulder, leaning his body into mine.

"You were going to say something, William?" I said. He coughed and reluctantly pulled away from me.

"Yes, yes," he replied, and we continued to walk. "Do you trust Gabriel again?"

"No. But I do have some concern for him. It is a hard realisation that the world you know it is an illusion," I replied. "Do you think I need to be worried about Vincenzo?"

"What? No. Absolutely not. But if it was anyone other than you I may say a little. He is an honourable man above all things, and would never do anything that could harm you in any way." William brushed a loose hair off my forehead. "I will not get into detail, but I can tell you with the utmost confidence that he has the situation under control. It's something he has had to manage for at least 80 years."

He laughed when my expression went blank. "You did not know? Your dear Gigi is one of the younger ones at 70. Have they not spoken of any of this? You too will age slowly and not have the pleasure of a traditional death."

"And you?"

"Oh no, my love. I am mortal enough that age will eventually catch up with me. But let's not concern ourselves with this now," he said. We turned and began back towards the house, where Gigi was waiting impatiently by the door.

"Apparently my Latin and Greek need work," I said when we saw her. "I am not sure if she believes The Old Ones will speak every known language or she has finally gone mad."

"Humour her. But if the need should arise, remind her that her Italian only improved when she began to teach you."

When we went into the kitchen Gabriel was hard at work. I watched him for several moments, waiting for a time to greet him, but he was so focused there was no chance. Gigi began to grow impatient so I went with her. I would make a point of finding him later.

"I don't think you are quite grasping how important making a good impression on Les Vieux is," Gigi began when we had returned to her room.

"Why would you say that?" I asked. "I just don't believe it necessary to be in a state of panic about it. We will do our best, as always."

She went to continue when I stopped her and asked, "May I tell you something you might find amusing?"

"I doubt it, but you can try."

"Do you remember when Natalia approached me? It was to ask me to speak to Charles on her behalf. To secure her place here."

She raised an eyebrow. "What on earth for? I thought...."

"Ah, you see, that is where we have all been mistaken. The girl has no wish to have relations. With anyone, let alone procreate."

"That is amusing."

"*And* she believes he will cast her out if she does not do as she wishes."

"So she asks *you* to speak to him?" Gigi began to laugh hysterically.

I frowned. "Why is *that* the funny part of it?"

"Oh petite, do not misunderstand me." Gigi took a few calming breaths. "It is very amusing that she would pick someone who is technically another's second. I am not trying to insult you but it is the truth. But thank you that did bring a smile to my face."

"So, I am of the opinion...," I started. She raised a finger in the air and I rolled my eyes.

"If you are so concerned about how we appear to Les Vieux it would be best if we did not mention this to Charles until things have settled." I stood and began the sentence in Latin, ending in Greek. "So you may not under any circumstances use it as a weapon against him. Promise me."

I tried to say 'madam' and ended up with something closer to mad, as in anger.

"Petite, please..."

"Promise me. This is too important, you said so yourself."

She huffed impatiently. "Alright! I promise. But I cannot guarantee when this is over that I will not laugh in his face."

"Did he try to impregnate you? When he found out you were dhampir I mean?" I asked.

"I absolutely refuse to answer that! What gives you the right to ask me such a horrendous question!" Her mood flipped to anger so quickly I was frightened. "I have been easy on you with your casual tone and intrusive questions but no more! If I wish to share something with you I will, you may no longer ask!"

Unsure if I should cry or get up and leave, I said nothing. She began to pace furiously around the room, her skin turning red as she ground her teeth. She kicked over a stack of letters that were on the floor beside her writing desk, letters I had not noticed, written on fancy paper with an elaborate red wax seal I did not recognise. She often had me help with her correspondence so I was surprised to see them.

"Leave," she said finally. I stood without another word and headed for the door.

"Practice your Latin and Greek elsewhere. If you perform badly Charles will be the very least of your worries."

THE LORDS WORDS

"Why do you suppose Grisela will not tell me? Does she know something terrible?" Sybilla asked. "I would hate for her to be upset with me."

"I am sure she is not. She is quite overwhelmed, with Les Vieux wanting the execution to be held here," I replied, when in truth I was unsure of exactly what Gigi was feeling. She had not spoken directly to me in several days.

Sybillia sighed and continued to hang costumes; we had agreed to help Josephine clean up the main room while she worked on some new pieces.

"So it is true that it shall be done on the stage. How horrible!" Sybilla exclaimed. "Do you know how it shall be carried out?"

"No, and I am glad. I quite enjoy uninterrupted sleep." I did not repeat what Vincezo had told me. I did not want to upset my friend.

"I must admit I am excited by the prospect of meeting my real father, if he is in fact one of Les Vieux. The Crown Prince never took much interest in me. Perhaps he knew all along I was not his." She spoke quickly. "If Gigi knew do you think she would tell me?"

I hesitated. "I do not know for certain, Sybilla. You would have to ask her."

"Is something troubling you, mon ami?"

"Many things, but nothing of consequence."

We heard the door to the underground that was closest to us slam and the sound of running footsteps. Natalia came clattering into the room like someone had been chasing her.

"What is the trouble?" I asked her as she caught her breath.

"You have spoken to Lord Westwick?" she asked.

"I have not had the opportunity to yet, but..."

"You must do *today*."

"Why?"

"*Please* Katrine, I beg you," she exclaimed, and then promptly burst into tears. I went to the girl and hugged her as she sobbed in my arms. She muttered quietly into my shoulder, begging me to help her and saying she was afraid.

"Please calm yourself, Natalia. You have no need to fear. I will speak to Charles today. You have my word." I pat her back slowly. She wailed and began to sob louder, her pleas becoming broken thank you in French and her native Russian.

When the girl finally recovered herself and left I turned back to what I was doing, Sybilla stood watching me, dumbfounded.

"Should I ask?" she said.

"Probably not. I will explain when I have a chance to resolve it."

There were several problems with me trying to speak to Charles, and I could not put myself in such a situation without a plan.

So when we returned to the chateau I went looking for Gigi.

I knocked on her door before entering; she was sitting at her writing desk with her back to the bedroom door.

"I apologise for disturbing you, Mademoiselle, but I need

your assistance," I said to her in Latin. She turned to me; one of those unknown letters lay open on her desk.

"What is it?" she asked. Her eyes were bloodshot as if she had been crying.

"I must speak with Charles now, Natalia came to me today quite frantic and I fear I can leave it no longer."

"So why come to me?"

"Because I cannot without your help. I know you are angry with me but this is very important."

She stood, smoothing down the skirt of her simple grey dress. She looked as if she had dressed herself in clothes from my closet.

"Are you alright, Mademoiselle?" I asked.

"Fine. I do not need to be glamorous to study," she replied in flawless Greek. "Now, let's get this over with."

"Katrine! Gigi! What a lovely surprise!" Charles exclaimed as we entered the library. I dismissed the servants and shut the door behind me. Gigi took a seat in one of the larger chairs.

Charles's eyes lowered. "I get the impression this is not a friendly visit."

"Do I have to speak Latin or Greek or will French suffice?" I asked Gigi.

She lowered her eyes at me. "Do as you like. This is on you."

"Good Lord, Katrine, are you with child?" he asked me, and I burst out laughing.

"Are you mad Charles?" Gigi laughed as well.

"I would have to be fornicating to be with child, unless I was the recipient of an immaculate conception." I stood close to him and made sure we made eye contact. "But I am here for just as serious of a matter, and I need you to give me your word that you will say nothing until I am finished. Can you do that?"

"Yes, of course. What's the trouble?" he said, his expression becoming greatly concerned.

"It's about Natalia." His expression went blank when I mentioned her name. "She is deeply troubled by the idea that if she does not have relations with you that you will toss her out. I tried to reassure her that you are not that sort of man, but she cares for you and worries you will be insulted. But at this time she has no wish to have relations with anyone, or have children. She asked me to speak with you because she is greatly concerned she will insult you."

I breathed a sigh of relief when I was finished, hoping I had done my best. Gigi nodded at me in silent approval.

"Is that it?" he asked.

"Pardon me?" I replied.

"Is that all, Katrine?"

He made me pause. I was quite speechless.

He turned to Gigi. "And what part do you have to play in this, Grisela?"

"She is my protégée, Charles. She would need my approval to act on such a matter, regardless of Natalia's state," Gigi said.

"So here is the trouble! Katrine has suddenly become obedient!" Charles exclaimed.

"My position in this company is not high, my Lord. Who says you would not dismiss me over such matters?" I replied.

He smiled. "Did I cast you aside when you refused my advances?"

Gigi snorted. "You wouldn't have dared!"

"So is everything alright?" I asked.

"I will reassure the girl that she is safe. Hopefully I can find a way to be rid of this womanising reputation." He smiled kindly at me, and I believed him.

Gigi began to laugh. "Why on earth would you do that when you so cherish it?"

"That's in *your* mind!" His angry voice made me jump. "But you so easily forget that *you* left me! I was your cast off, not the other way around!"

He stormed out of the library. I had never seen him so angry.

I kept my eyes lowered so I would not make eye contact with Gigi. I did not want to do anything that would trouble her mood.

Gigi stood and crossed the room. I stood perfectly still as she approached me.

"Tonight is the last performance, and Les Vieux will be present," she said calmly. "I expect no less then perfection. Do you understand?"

"Yes, Madam," I said quickly in Latin after failing to find the proper words in Greek. I bowed to her as she left the room, closing the door behind her.

I could not even process what had just happened. Only that Natalia was safe.

Les Vieux was close. I had to prepare.

OUTCAST

Hannah was pacing when I returned to my room. She had a dark blue gown laid out on the bed.

"What on earth is that?" I asked, pointing at the dress. "I am in mourning."

"It sounds as if not anymore. That dress was specifically chosen by Mademoiselle Delphine and I have been ordered to put aside your mourning wear," Hannah replied. She looked quite stressed.

I smiled at her. "How long do we have?"

Her expression eased with relief. "Not long. You are not angry?"

"It sounds as if I am no longer allowed to decide anything for myself," I replied as she helped me undress. "My role has now become a silent one."

"Do you know the source of this sudden anger?" Hannah asked as she pulled the dress on me. It was beautiful midnight blue silk trimmed with black lace.

"It is nice to see you in colour again, Katrine," Hannah added.

"Thank you. I do not know specifically why Gigi is so angry, only that I seem to be receiving the brunt of it." I did not look her in the eye as I spoke for fear that I would cry.

"We always hurt the ones we love," Hannah said.

"I sure hope so, or I may not survive the night."

William was standing off by himself, looking very angry, when I came down the stairs. He usually came to wish me good luck but he appeared to be keeping his distance. I went to go to him when I heard Gigi call my name sharply.

"I will say goodbye to William," I said flatly to her.

"You will do as you are told," Gigi snapped. "Your relationship is unseemly and *I insist it stop immediately!*"

I stopped, and I felt everyone around hold their breath in anticipation. Charles, Natalia, Victorie and Vincenzo were present, along with several servants and Morgana came in from the salon.

"No," I said. I moved so I was standing face to face with her, trying to remain calm.

"Pardon me? Do you forget your place, girl? You would be nothing if it were not for me." Gigi looked down on me as she spoke, her angry words like venom.

"For which I am grateful, but I will not be treated like some lesser being because you are in a foul mood."

"How dare you!"

"Dare I what? Ask for you to mistreat the person you are truly angry with? That is merely common courtesy, Mademoiselle. If you are so dissatisfied with me I shall leave this house at once and you will never see me again," I declared. "But you will *under no circumstances* take away the man I love."

Gigi came at me, raising her hand to strike me. "You are my protégée and I shall do with you as I wish!"

"Perhaps, but you have no authority to throw anyone out of this company," Charles said, stepping between us. "So whatever your displeasure may be, Katrine will not be leaving unless I say so."

Gigi began to say something but Charles continued, "You have gone on as if you are Queen of the Realm for far too long. Either you control your attitude or you will be stripped of your privileges."

She turned and stormed out. I bit the inside of my cheek to stop myself from crying.

"Thank you, Charles," I said when I heard the clatter of hooves and knew she wasn't coming back.

"Think nothing of it, she is being ridiculous," he replied. "Just promise me you won't run off now, will you?"

I smiled a weak smile. "I promise."

He took Natalia's arm and they went out to his carriage, Natalia smiled happily and winked at me on their way out. Even though I was shaken, it pleased me to see things had worked out for her.

I felt William's hand link with mine at my side. I had not realised I was shaking.

Vincenzo stood on my other side, staring out the door. I watched him carefully; I wanted to reach out to him but restrained myself.

"What should I do?" I asked him.

"Nothing," His gaze remained forward. "I always thought you would be better suited for my line of work than this 'proper lady' business."

I stayed silent, unsure of what to do with myself. I had not really entertained the thought of my place not being with Gigi.

"I shall protect you, Katrine. I am the one who found you, do not forget that," Vincenzo told me, his finger pointing at my face. "Now, unless you are planning on not performing tonight we should go."

I nodded in agreement, and he, William and I rode out to the theatre.

I kept William's hand firmly in mine until we reached the door to the underground. When our eyes met I had no doubt I had done the right thing.

I would not lose him. Not for anything.

"I love you, Katrine," he said softly into my ear when he pulled me into his arms.

"I love you, William. I am sorry we cannot leave, but I had to promise Charles," I replied.

He laughed loudly, brushing my loose hair behind my ear. "That is quite alright. I am sure our time will come."

I quickly changed into my costume and went up to the stage, being careful not to speak or look directly at anyone. I was sure word of my humiliation had spread throughout the company by now and I could not hide from the stares, so I tried my best to ignore them.

Gigi barked orders at the other dancers like an angry dictator, I was sure the audience could hear yelling from beyond the closed curtain. I kept my eyes down and Gigi was noticeably silent as she walked past me and exited the stage.

A fury of whispers began, not about me but about the private box beside Charles's where Les Vieux would be seated.

It seemed ironic to me that they were sitting where the individual who they had come to execute once sat.

The performance went well but not flawlessly, the audience did not notice but I was certain Gigi would be furious. Thankfully the mistake was not mine, or Sybilla's, and that was all I cared about.

"Do you think they shall come back to the salon?" Sybilla asked as we changed.

"I do not know. I suppose." I shrugged my shoulders, not

looking at her as I spoke.

"Are you alright, Katrine?"

"Why do you ask?"

She frowned. "I heard what happened. I did not want to ask you outright. I hope I did not upset you further."

"No, no, mon ami. It is quite alright. I would have been lost without Vincenzo and I am grateful to Charles for protecting me."

"So what shall you do with yourself if you are no longer..."

"I am not ready to discuss that. That is not my all I am, I can survive on my own." I was sharper with her then I had intended to be, but I was still upset.

Sybilla seemed startled. "I am sorry if I upset you, but I am concerned. If you were to leave I would follow."

"I promised Charles I would not."

"I am sorry to ask, but will you be by my side when we meet Les Vieux? I cannot bare it on my own. I am so nervous!"

I smiled at her, and I was reminded of when I was about to go and meet the Countess for the first time. I flushed with the memory of how nervous I was.

"Of course," I said, holding my hand out to her. "I will stay by your side, no matter what happens."

William was waiting for us when we came upstairs, and he escorted us out quickly to Vincenzo's waiting carriage.

"Les Vieux are coming to the salon." Vincenzo informed us once we were all inside. "They were impressed with the show."

I chuckled. "Gigi must be pleased."

"Perhaps her reign of terror will cease after all the praise she will receive tonight," Vincenzo continued. "But do not fret, my dear. Your life will not stop if she releases you. I will teach you all that I know, if need be."

I smiled at him. "Then I will be a well rounded woman indeed."

"I apologise if this is my fault," William said.

"Tis not, my love." I squeezed his hand.

"If you all are to leave, I wish to come along," Sybilla chimed in.

Vincenzo smiled at her. "Of course, and I am sure Morgana would also. But Katrine has promised Charles so we must stay till Les Vieux leave, then we could go on an extended trade mission if necessary. I am sure Charles would support another branch of the Danse Macabre somewhere else if something intriguing should arise."

"You are very kind, Signor, to go to such lengths for Katrine," Sybilla said.

"I will do what I need to keep her close to me," Vincenzo replied, squeezing my knee. "I must warn you, your cousin is beside himself about this mess with Grisela, Katrine. So please indulge him. I tried to reassure him that you would be alright, but he has not been the same since that night you saw your Grandmother's daughter."

The carriage finally stopped and Tolone and Hannah were waiting on the steps of the chateau.

"Are you well, Mademoiselle?" Hannah asked. I knew she was being formal because others were present, but I could see in her eyes she was deeply concerned.

"I am, Hannah. If something changes I will tell you otherwise," I told her. "And you will be taking orders from me or Signor Amori from now on."

Her eyes sparkled with joy but her face remained expressionless. "Yes, madam."

She helped me inside and took my cloak; it was important that she knew that she would stay with me, regardless of what happened. I nodded to her before she turned to walk away.

"I should like to have tea when I retire to my room," I said to her, a quiet signal that we would speak further later.

"Of course," she replied, quickly leaving with the other

servants as we walked in to the salon.

There were three men and two women I did not recognise speaking to Gigi and Charles, they turned only for a moment as we entered the room.

But one man's eyes stayed on us as we approached, he kept glancing at Sybilla. His amber eyes were stunning against his pale skin and long dark hair. He was handsome with well chiselled features.

I sensed Gabriel coming up behind us and held out my hand to him.

"You belong with me," he said sharply in my ear. "I will protect you. I do not know what the Order wants with our family but I will find out."

"Cousin, please. We have friends here, and you do not need to worry. We will stay together, I promise." I leaned towards him to whisper and gently kissed his cheek.

"Wonderful!" Charles exclaimed when he saw us. "May I introduce to you Signor Vincenzo Amori, William of Naples, and Mademoiselle Katrine Bathory and her cousin, Gabriel. And, of course, one of our newest members, Sybilla."

"Lord Bathory, it is an honour," the olive skinned woman said, her dark eyes clear and penetrating. She wore a white gown that draped beautifully over her body, her thick dark hair hanging long around her shoulders.

"My name is Anai," she said, extending her hand. "This woman is Suren, and these men are Thaddeus, Finn Hawk, and Prince Radu Dracula."

Gabriel bowed, pulling me down with him. I had a flash of when Roza and I were first brought before him.

Rising up to make eye contact with the man, Gabriel said, "Prince Radu, we are humbled by your presence. I was also once Prince of Wallachia and my cousin grew up there."

Radu smiled, bowing also. "Then it is an honour, for fellow Prince's do not often meet unless on the battlefield. Where in Wallachia are you from, Lady Bathory?"

"Arefu, my Lord." It had been a long time since I had spoke the name of my home.

"So you know Castle Poenari, my brother's stronghold?" Radu asked.

"I could see it from my village," I replied, and it finally sunk in who he was. His brother was a hero, a great man who drove the Turks from Wallachia.

"Splendid," he said, stepping closer to Sybilla. "So it is no wonder that my seed would find you. Come closer, child, so I may examine your face."

Sybilla stepped forward, looking quite nervous. She looked at Gabriel and I, clearly quite frightened. I tried to smile reassuringly at her. Radu took her chin between his two fingers.

The blonde burly man who they called Finn Hawk laughed loudly. "*This* is the girl, Radu?"

"I do not understand," Sybilla said as he gazed at her face.

"I am your father, Sybilla. What is there to understand?" Radu asked. "You are Dracul. I am amazed that Ralmolunda never told you. She was very proud."

"She said you were Turkish." Sybilla managed to say. She was clearly quite shocked.

"I may as well be! I spent my formative years with the Turks," he exclaimed. "But, that is for another time."

The lady called Suren smiled warmly. "It is lovely to meet you all. You girls performed wonderfully tonight. It was like nothing I had ever seen."

Suren had glossy black hair that was tied back in a tight plait and she had unusually shaped eyes. She has dressed in long black robes trimmed in gold.

"Something wrong, Lady Bathory?" Suren asked me.

"No, not at all. You are just so unique looking," I replied.

"I quite like your outfit."

"I am sure you have never seen another of my kind," Suren said. "And you may never again. But do not worry, I am used to stares. I come from quite far; my people are loyal to the Khan's. We do not travel much to this part of Europe."

Thaddeus, the other man, said nothing, he just stood silently and watched us with sharp eyes. He was tall and lean with close cropped dark hair and an angular face.

"We are honoured that you were able to come to one of our performances, and most pleased that you enjoyed it," Charles said. "If there is anything we can do to make your stay more comfortable, do not hesitate to ask."

"You are the victim of the Von Dores girl's first attack, Lady Bathory?" Suren asked me.

"Yes, and I will be quite pleased when this is all over," I said.

"Let us reassure you that justice will be carried out." Finn Hawk told me rather abruptly, his voice was very deep and stern.

"Thank you," I replied.

Prince Radu clasped his hands together. "Enough of that talk. Shall we dance?"

I sat with Sybilla while the others danced; she was so overwhelmed she could barely form a sentence. I would not, could not, look at Gigi; but when I felt her eyes turn to me from the dance floor I thought I might vomit.

Now that I had a moment to think I was in a state of shock.

"I suppose when they were warning you about me someone should have warned you about her. I am so sorry, Katrine," Charles said softly as he pulled a chair up beside me. "People are nothing to her, disposable like used undergarments. You did not, and do not, deserve it. I am true to my word. Your place is with us now, regardless of what she says. I hope you know that, and I know you are heartbroken now but it will pass."

I smiled at him, and I could not hide my tears. "Will you tell me one day?"

"Tell you what?"

"About the two of you. Will you tell me one day?"

He shrugged his shoulders. "I suppose I owe you that. I promise that she will not be allowed to hurt you anymore."

"Thank you. Your words have brought me comfort." I smiled and nodded, even though I wanted desperately to run to my bed and sob. When my eyes turned back to the crowd Victorie had entered and Les Vieux seemed excited. Thaddeus embraced her as if they were old friends.

Charles looked rather confused.

"Is something wrong?" I asked.

"The story always was that there was more to Victorie then any of us knew but *that* I did not expect." Charles watched Victorie as she conversed with Les Vieux, clearly quite confused.

He stayed with us, sitting in silence as we watched the others dance. Never in my life did I think that I would find the presence of Lord Charles Westwick comforting but I did, and he stayed close by until I rose to leave. Sybilla followed, we said our goodnights then went our separate ways.

There were tea and sweet cakes in my room; Hannah was muddling about trying to look busy.

I closed my door and I felt my body begin to shake. Hannah quickly crossed the room and pulled me into her arms as I began to sob.

"Do not worry, child," Hannah said quietly to me. "You have real friends here. You will be taken care of."

"Did she try to fire you?" I asked.

Hannah snorted. "*Tried*, yes. But Signor Amori put her in her place."

"What do you mean?"

"He pays my salary, child, not her! She covered some of your expenses, but not all. I was one of those things," she replied. "He even told me in front of her that if she tries anything to not only tell him immediately but to refuse to her face! She was furious!"

I wiped my tears on my sleeve. "I do not know what I would do without him."

"Let us pray that you never have to find out. The opinion of Lord Westwick throughout the household has also changed. I did not think he had it in him."

I smiled. "Vincenzo believes I may be better suited to work with him then being a proper lady. I am not sure exactly what Gigi had planned for me but I think I could still be a lady and work. Perhaps there is room for both."

"I am sure he did not mean that you should behave like a Neanderthal while working with him." She put her hand on my shoulder as she spoke. "And, if I may speak freely, I believe Mademoiselle Delphine's way of life is growing old and tired, and that women will start to behave like men soon enough, having their own jobs and free thinking like we are meant to. The world is changing, Katrine, and perhaps it is best to change right along with it."

She began to help me change, and as the layers began to be removed exhaustion set in. I felt my shoulders slump.

"It will all work out for the best, I am sure of it," Hannah said. "Sometimes things fall apart because they are an improper fit, and when you put them back together they are stronger than before."

She pulled the dress over my head. I helped myself to tea and cakes as she put things away. I put a double dose of blood in my tea, and had drunk two cups before she returned. She poured herself a cup of tea and sat on the bed beside me.

"For what it's worth, I would not have allowed her to fire you, Hannah. I would not have stood for it." My sadness felt like added weight to my limbs.

She smiled. "I know, and thank you. I hope your loyalty isn't further exploited."

WELCOME VISITOR

I opened my eyes only slightly, startled when I saw someone sitting in the darkness. I sat up and wiped the sleep from my eyes, sure they were playing tricks on me.

"Who's there?" I called out into the night.

The woman shuffled in her seat, her skirts sounding like rustling feathers.

"It is only me, my sweet Katrine," my Grandmother said as I lit the small taper I kept by my bed.

"I am so pleased to see you, Grandmother. My world fell apart when I heard the news of...."

"You were probably the only person in this world who thought twice about it." She looked at me with such warmth I felt immediately loved. I was surprised to see that she was wearing the outfit from the portrait I had seen in Csejthe; a brown velvet dress with puffy white sleeves and a wide, stiff lace collar that framed her face, her hair pulled up in a net with pearls.

"I am sure Gabriel...I mean, I am sure Gabor would argue that fact," I told her.

Her expression brightened. "How is my cousin fairing?"

"He is overwhelmed, some business with the Order of the Dragon. But he is doing well otherwise."

"And how are you, child?"

"Better now that you are here. Can you tell me about your daughter, Anna?"

She tilted her head, her dark eyes twinkling. "Why do you wish to know about Anna?"

"She approached me and asked Gabor to leave with her. I wanted to know something about her and her relationship with him. He is quite distraught."

"I am not surprised, he and Anna were very close as children," she replied, a slight smirk on her face. "My Anna will deny being anything like me, but she always reminded me of my mother. She loved her father so. She has some cold indifference, but when she is passionate she is fiery and forceful. She is smart and sharp in a way not expected of a woman, but lacks the compassion of her younger siblings. She is her father's daughter."

She sighed, and then continued. "She will have difficulty accepting you, she was most disturbed by the crimes I was said to have committed."

"She is one of us now. I hope that will change her mind about some things."

"What do you mean 'one of you'?"

I stared at her face, the feelings I'd had when I'd first seen her came flooding back. I did not want her to be angry, and I did not want to break her heart.

"Someone has turned her. She gave up her mortal life," I said. Her expression did not change, but the sparkle in her eyes faded.

"Do you know the circumstances?" she asked. "I mean, do you know how, or..."

"I am sorry. I do not."

She put her hand to her mouth, stifling a sob. She quickly regained her composure, her expression going flat.

"Tell me about your life. Is Grisela Delphine good to you?"

"I can read and write in multiple languages, including French, Italian, Latin and Greek, and speak all with relative ease. I've learned manners and am constantly improving my etiquette. I can dance, and soon I will be joining trade missions."

"Trade? Really? I did not know Mademoiselle Delphine did such things."

I smiled. "She doesn't. This is something I will learn from another, and I am quite excited."

I could not, would not tell her what Gigi had done. I could not find a way to explain where it did not sound as if I had been cast off in disgrace.

"I am so pleased to hear the world has evolved in such a manner that a woman can do such a job without discrimination. I am proud of you." She reached out to me, cupping my chin with one hand and running the thumb of her other hand along my jaw line.

My heart sank as I looked into her eyes, she smiled affectionately at me.

"You grow more beautiful every time I see you," she said. "Gabor is involved in your care?"

"Of course. As much as he can be. He needs to have his own life."

"As long as you are part of each other's lives I am overjoyed. I trust him unconditionally."

"He is overwhelmed with guilt that he could not help you. I think he feels responsible for what happened to you in the end." I pulled my blanket up closer to my chest. "I am also bothered that I could do nothing for you."

She snorted. "He was better equipped then you were. He had an army who betrayed him, a heinous crime. I hope all of those men are slaughtered. Please make sure he knows I do not blame him."

"Yes, Grandmother, I will."

"You are but a girl, Katrine. Destroying my journal was the

greatest thing you could have done for me. Now that Anna has found you, I pray that she can find a way to accept you. It would bring me such joy."

TAINT

The dream of my Grandmother was still fresh in my mind when Hannah woke me the next morning.

"Today you will go with Signor Amori," Hannah said. "He asked for you to be well fed for it may be a long day."

I was overcome with joy. "Believe it or not I am quite looking forward to this."

"I am excited to hear about your new adventure," Hannah replied, I could see the strain in her face. I did not think she would have such trouble with my unconventional new life. She put a tray with tea and some food in front of me; I reached out and grabbed her hand.

"It will be alright, Hannah. I am sure of it," I said. She smiled, and then went back to readying my clothes.

Preparing to leave the house for the day had become much less complicated.

"Perhaps we will travel," I began, "in a way that is less.... disruptive then the way we travelled to Russia. Vincenzo was telling me about..."

"As a young woman you could just go along with the men?"

Her question caused me to pause. "I suppose I shall have to

say I am someone's wife, since I no longer have a defined position. I shall be William's wife one day..."

She giggled, and then stopped herself rather abruptly.

"What's so funny?" I asked.

"So what shall we call you, then? Will you have a married name or shall you become Madam of Naples?" She giggled again. "Introductions would become very strange."

"I will ask him, but for the most part I will stay Katrine Bathory. It was not long ago that I received the name, I am not going to lose it again so quickly," I replied. "Now that I think of it, I wonder why I do not know his family name."

"I don't think anyone does, dear. Do not be alarmed."

I ate until I thought I may explode, taking a generous amount of blood in my tea. I felt quite good when I finally went downstairs to find Vincenzo so we could get going.

Gigi stood in the front entry way, on the opposite side of the room from Vincenzo and William, her arms crossed across her chest. She stared angrily at me as I came down the stairs and put on my travelling cloak; I tried my best to pretend I did not see her. The men nodded at me and we started out the door.

Gigi began to cuss loudly in Italian, following us out into the street. She kept going on about Vincenzo's ultimate betrayal, and how she would never forgive him for it. He did not say a word, did not even turn his eyes in her direction as we got in the carriage and left her standing in the street.

"I am so sorry," was all I could think to say to him. I tried to breathe calmly to stop myself from crying.

"Why? She was like this long before you came along. This is quite common for her," Vincenzo replied.

"Then why was I not told sooner?"

He hesitated for a moment. "Because we all believed that if she would take on a protégée after all this time that something had changed, that genuinely caring for another's welfare had done something miraculous for her. But apparently we were wrong, and I apologise."

"But it was not only Gigi that took you on, and I am not so flippant," he continued. "I cannot teach you about female topics, but I do not entirely believe that all of those things need to be taught. I hope you will learn some practical life skills from me that you can use to exist in this ever evolving world."

"I am quite looking forward to it," I said, then turned to William. "May I ask what your family name is?"

"You may ask but that does not mean I will tell you," he replied with a big smile.

"But you will have to, eventually, because I will not be referred to as Madam of Naples when we are married. That is just nonsense."

William began to laugh quite hysterically while Vincenzo and I stared at him.

"She has a point, mon ami," Vincenzo said to him.

"I figured she would be too preoccupied with Gigi to think of such things," William replied, looking back and forth at our blank expressions. "What? You cannot tell me that you both don't find it amusing."

When we didn't reply, he continued. "Besides, I did not think you would be willing to give up the Bathory name so easily. Noblewomen do not often take their husbands name. I am sure your Grandmother only used her husband's name once she was widowed."

I remembered when I first told my story to Vincenzo and Gigi I had presented my Grandmother as the Lady Widow Nadasdy, and Gigi had immediately called her Countess Bathory. Perhaps there was some truth to what he was saying.

"Before we arrive I must explain some things to you, Katrine," Vincenzo told me. "We are going to retrieve an artefact from an old witch, and her daughter. They believe it to be worthless and it needs to remain that way."

"What sort of thing warrants such deception?" I asked.

"Do you remember me speaking to you of alchemy?"

"Only briefly, yes."

"Well, this tool, which was once widely used by witches, is now extremely useful to alchemists, and if the witches found out they would hide them or price them so high they would be quite out of reach. So, you understand?"

I smiled. "Yes, of course. I suppose when we leave you can tell me what the object is?"

"I will try my best," Vincenzo replied.

We arrived at an outdoor market on the banks of the Seine. I wondered if we were close to Vincenzo's office. There were crowds of people buying food stuffs, I immediately gravitated to the breads and baked goods while the men moved on ahead of me. I tried to stay close to them while observing my surroundings.

"I loved her with my entire being," a female voice said from behind me. I turned just as Countess Zrinyi took off her hood.

"Excuse me, my lady, but I do not understand." I hid my hands so she could not seem them shaking.

"I have thought quite frequently about our last encounter, and I realised that I may not have been entirely clear about some things," she said, staring intently at my face. "I may be ashamed of what my mother has done, but she is still my mother and one of the greatest who ever lived and I love her. I will always love her; she meant everything to my siblings and I. I thought you needed to know that."

"Thank you for sharing that with me. To be honest, I never once doubted how any of your family felt about her," I replied. We stared silently at each other for what seemed like a very long time; the way she titled her head, her penetrating gaze, the way she used her hands was almost identical to my Grandmother. I watched as she pushed a loose strand of hair off her forehead and was immediately drawn back to that room in Csejthe.

"I wanted to apologise to you, in part, because I cannot imagine what it is like for you. The taint of being a bastard is not easy to shake," she said.

"Some wear it like a badge of honour," I said proudly. I did not point out to her that I was not the bastard, my mother was. It seemed like an inappropriate time. Perhaps when it came to nobility such a label carried on from a parent.

She chuckled. "That is something that takes a lot of bravery. I do not think I could do it. Perhaps that is why my cousin wishes to remain close to you. But when the time comes, he will join me. And perhaps you shall also."

"I suppose we shall just have to wait and see." I smiled kindly at her, trying to maintain the tone of the conversation.

William called my name, Countess Zrinyi smirked at me just as I turned my head, and when I looked back she was gone.

"Something wrong?" William asked as he came up beside me. I scanned the crowd but there was no sign of Countess Zrinyi.

"No," I replied, taking his arm and continuing on.

We came to a small wood cart that had large fish stacked on it; the smell was so overwhelming it felt like it was absorbing into my skin. The old woman was hunched over the side speaking quietly to Vincenzo while the younger woman, who I assumed was her daughter, tried to sell the fish.

Both glanced briefly at us but focused mainly on William. I wondered if they could sense what he was.

"I still do not understand why you desire such meaningless object, Signor," the old woman said in French.

He chuckled. "It is merely for decoration. My client is only pleased with pretty things."

The old woman glanced at me and laughed. "Yes, young women have such fickle desires. I have it for you today along with a small piece of information which I will share with you at no charge."

Vincenzo nodded and they exchanged packages, she leaned over and whispered something into his ear. I saw a twinkle in his eye but his expression remained blank.

"Merci, Madam. That is a most interesting revelation," Vincenzo said to her. They said their goodbyes, the young woman continued to stare at William.

"Is she a friend of yours?" I asked once we were out of earshot.

"Who?" William said casually.

"The young one was watching you like she was familiar with you intimately."

He chuckled. "Let me assure you I only have knowledge of both of those women as Vincenzo's contacts, my love. But you must understand, when she looks at me she sees power and the potential for powerful offspring. Think of it like Charles and Natalia."

"That is quite vile."

"But not uncommon among the races. Do not be surprised if Sybilla acquires a new group of admirers as well. Especially when she is seen with Prince Radu."

Vincenzo shuffled quickly passed us, motioning for us to move faster. He did not look panicked but there seemed to be some urgency.

He seemed to breathe easy again once we were in the carriage.

"So what did she tell you?" William asked before I could say anything.

"You would not believe me if I told you." Vincenzo smiled to himself.

"Vincenzo, you're practically giddy."

"She said someone has developed a cure for the thirst."

I felt my eyebrows rise. "The thirst for..."

"For blood, Katrine." He looked at me like I was a foolish child.

"You're joking," I said.

"No I am afraid I'm not," he replied. "I would have ignored it had I not been told the same story a week ago, and had she not said a name I know."

"So what do we do?"

"We keep this between us," Vincenzo snapped.

"Why?" William asked.

"Because Charles will have us packed and gone before we have a chance to investigate."

William and I nodded in agreement; there was no arguing with Vincenzo's logic. Another journey was not appealing at the moment.

Vincenzo unwrapped the object carefully and handed it to me.

"What is it?" I asked, closely examining the brass plate. It was covered in embossed images with a large sun in the centre.

"It took a considerable amount of skill to make such an object," I explained as I ran my fingertips over the intricate patterns.

"You know about metal work?" Vincenzo asked.

"My father was...is an enameller by trade, like his father before him. And my brother after him, I suppose." I felt the corners of my mouth rise as I thought of Bodi. It had been a long time since I had thought much about my brother, or my father.

Vincenzo smiled. "If I knew that I had forgotten, I apologise. It could be rather useful in the future, that knowledge."

Before I could reply he continued. "The object is, essentially, the centrepiece of the witch's altar. They were believed to contain power, and being passed through the generations there was a story that it held the powers of the ancestors. I am not entirely sure how it happened but someone proved it false so the plates are being disposed of. Alchemists are taking any cast offs from magical beings that they can, you would have to ask them why."

"It's a shame they don't keep them simply because they have been in the family for so long, as part of their legacy," I said.

"Some are not as sentimental as you, mon ami," Vincenzo replied.

"I suppose when one loses their family they become concerned with such things."

The carriage stopped, and I looked out the window to see we were back at the chateau.

"Can we go somewhere else?" I asked.

Vincenzo rolled his eyes. "She's gone to the theatre. I believe the execution is tomorrow."

Tolone opened the door and we stepped out onto the street, Vincenzo had rewrapped the object and he handed it to Tolone.

"When was I to be told?" I asked no one in particular.

"Now that you are no longer...," William started, pausing as he examined my expression, "what I mean is, because it was usually covered by someone else we were unsure of the best approach."

He took my hand and squeezed it, then pulled me into a hug.

"It will be over quickly, and then we can move on. There is a whole world full of opportunities that we can explore together," he said quietly into my ear.

"It sounds as if you are pleased that I have been cast off." I immediately regretted it after I said it. He pulled away, keeping his hands on my shoulders as he examined my face.

"I only want what's best for you, il mio amore."

ONLY GOD CAN JUDGE ME

Silence and tension hung over the chateau like a dark cloud preparing to burst with rain. The execution would take place at sundown so we could all be present. Those of us who were up in the day had to sit around and wait for the time to arrive, which was torture in itself.

But I was not good at waiting, so I wandered the chateau trying to clear my head.

Gigi ambushed me as I was about to leave the library.

"You must be quite pleased with yourself," she began, leaning against the door frame so her body blocked the exit.

"If I knew about what I had done to anger you I could better answer that question." I stood back far enough that I was out of her reach.

"So are you screwing all three of them or just Charles? No, you have to be on Vincenzo's feeding schedule for him to behave in such a way. But I must admit I am surprised that William would share you." She smiled, tilting her head to one side. "Poor Gabriel will be so ashamed."

I returned her expression as best I could. "If that is the filthy lie you need to tell yourself to make yourself feel better, go ahead.

You've clearly made up your mind."

"And what would your Grandmother say?" she added. Without a second thought I was flying at her and had my hands around her throat. I squeezed, surprised at how easily I could crush her windpipe.

"Say what you like about me, but if you speak my Grandmother's name again I will tear your throat out." My voice was calmer then my insides felt.

She did not move. Her expression never changed. I had no idea what had happened that would make her turn away from me so easily.

Charles has said she does these sorts of things to people. As I looked into her eyes something inside me just snapped.

I turned and tossed her by the neck back into the room, not watching to see where she landed. Vincenzo was at the top of the stairs, as if he was coming to help. He watched me silently as I walked past him and made my way outside.

"She's just trying to hurt you," he said. Until he spoke I had not realised he'd followed me.

"She has impeccable timing," I said as I continued walking. I slowed down for only a moment so he could catch up.

"A key virtue for any decent courtesan," he replied. "She chooses her words carefully for the maximum impact. Whether they are true or she really means it seems to be irrelevant."

"She said Gabriel will be ashamed, and my Grandmother.... she said the only way I could be protected by you was if I was 'screwing' you and on your feeding schedule. She also said I must be 'screwing' Charles, and how could William share." I kept my eyes forward as I explained every horrible detail.

He ran his hand threw his hair. "I am so sorry, Katrine."

"The sad thing is that *I have no idea what 'screwing' means!*" I exclaimed, bursting into tears. He hugged me; the soft fabric of his jacket and the rumble of his chest were soothing. The warmth of his body wrapped around me and I felt safe.

"What exactly does she mean by 'screwing'?" I asked into his chest.

"She means sexual relations, I believe."

I pulled away a little so I could see his face. "She cannot be serious! What if she tells *Gabriel* that...that...she *cannot* be serious!"

He stroked my hair as I leaned back into him. "She's just trying to upset you, like today won't be hard enough. Now, come inside and we shall have tea in the conservatory. William is collecting Morgana and I believe we should discuss what is going to happen tonight."

I nodded in agreement, taking his arm as we went back inside.

***

William learned forward and our eyes met. "It is not as bad as it sounds."

Morgana chuckled. "Clearly you have never seen slaughter."

I rested my chin on my hands with my elbows on my knees. I had said very little as Vincenzo had explained, in a flat and emotionless way, what would take place and how we were expected to behave.

"Whatever it is, keep it to yourself until we are away from Les Vieux," Vincenzo said. "This is part of law and order in our world, ladies. You do not have to like it, and it will be easier on us all if you appeared indifferent."

I sighed loudly. "I will do my best."

"Gigi will mind her manners in front of Les Vieux, Katrine. So do not worry in that regard. And..."

"I will deal with what she says. I will speak to Gabriel. We had a scuffle, and if that does not deter her then she will have to suffer the consequences." I did not bother to hide my annoyance.

90

If Gigi wanted to fight with me, I would not back down.

"Should I ask?" William asked. Morgana raised her eyebrows as if she was wondering the same thing. Before I could continue Hannah came to the door of the conservatory.

"It's time," Hannah said nervously, her face was expressionless but she was wringing a cloth in her hands.

"Thank you, Hannah," I replied, watching her linger in the doorway before saying, "and you will not be needed so you can remain here."

She sighed in relief and her face softened. "Thank you, Mademoiselle."

She left quickly, I assumed before I could change my mind. I would not have subjected her to such things, I was not even sure the servants were allowed.

I did not wait for the men to escort me, I simply stood and left the room and knew they would follow.

The entryway was quite busy. It appeared that people were standing back waiting for Gigi to leave. She was taking her time putting on her gloves as if waiting for something.

Charles stood off to the side with Natalia, they were ready to leave and Charles was getting impatient. Sybilla came to stand with us; she looked lovely in black trimmed with silver embroidery. Her hair was up and in a net, it was the most dressed up I had ever seen her.

"Am I alright? Hannah helped me dress," Sybilla asked.

"You are lovely, so do not worry. Your dress is exquisite. I am pleased to hear Hannah has helped you." I was quite proud that my maid had done such a lovely job. Hannah had picked out a lovely grey outfit for me; now that I did not have my every move planned I could return to my mourning wear if I wished.

As Gigi lifted her head and looked around the room I ducked behind Vincenzo so she could not see me. I'd had enough of her for today.

Finally she left, and the room began to bustle with activity as we all rushed to leave. Sybilla came in Vincenzo's carriage with us. I was overjoyed to have all my closest friends together at this moment.

Charles led the way as we all mounted the stairs, coming to the theatre as a group. The black cloaked figures that flanked each doorway made the place seem unfamiliar.

"Who are they?" I whispered to Vincenzo as we went to the main room and sat down. I had never been in this position before, being able to view the stage from the audience's perspective.

"Mercenaries. Bounty hunters....hired help, for extra security it seems," he replied. He sat on my right and William, Morgana and Sybilla to my left. William clutched tightly to my hand.

"Hello cousin," Gabriel had taken a seat just behind me. His touch on my shoulder was soothing.

"Hello cousin. I am happy to see you," I said, smiling.

He leaned over and whispered to me, "Do not worry. I do not believe a word of that filth that woman has said to me."

"Thank you. That means a lot," I replied.

We were all finally seated and Prince Radu took the stage. He and Sybilla had had tea, and she was quite pleased with the conversation they'd had.

"Good evening, good people of the Danse Macabre!" he proclaimed. "Before we begin we must pay our sincerest respects to Alienor, whose presence was a joyous surprise! We have missed you greatly and wish you continued health and happiness!"

Victorie raised her hand and waved, the entire room shifted to look at her and I heard some small sounds that sounded like gasps.

"Who is Alienor?" I asked Vincenzo.

"Charles always said there was more to her story than any of us knew, but by the look on his face *he* did not even expect that,"

Vincenzo replied, pointing at a gape mouthed Charles who sat a few rows ahead.

Our attention quickly turned back to the stage as we heard the sound of chains dragging across wood. Even though two cloaked figures held Klara a few feet off the ground the shackles around her ankles still dragged as they brought her on the stage. I felt Gigi cringe at the possibility of marks on the wood crossed my mind.

Klara was set down but the figures guarding her remained, her sunken eyes scanned the crowd until they found Charles. From where we sat I could not hear her, but by the expression on her face she was clearly pleading for her life.

Anai came forward from the back of the stage and hit Klara, closed fist, in the face. Blood began to trickle from her nose.

"Lord Westwick is no longer in control!" she yelled. "You are *our* prisoner! If you must plead, do so to us!"

Klara nodded and lowered her head, her shoulders moving slightly as she cried.

"Klara Von Dores, you have committed heinous crimes, jeopardising your own kind and our way of life," Prince Radu proclaimed. "Your reckless actions have destroyed the lives of the men you enchanted and threatened exposure of us all. What say you?"

I silently prayed as I watched her, thankfully she did not say a word.

"Do you accept the authority of Les Vieux and their ability to pass judgment?" Prince Radu asked.

At that, Klara looked up at him and with an evil, nasty snarl she shouted, "No!"

She began to laugh in such a way the hair on the back of my neck stood up, saying in her regular voice, "Only God can judge me."

The other members of Les Vieux stepped forward. Finn Hawk was holding a mallet and Suren a large axe.

Prince Radu took the mallet from Finn Hawk. "Perhaps he

will be kind to you before he banishes you to hell."

Thaddeus held Klara's head as Radu swung, smashing Klara's teeth and quite possibly her jaw bone. Klara groaned in agony and the horrible crunching sound continued as he used the mallet to knock out all her teeth. Thaddeus then leaned her forward so she could spit the mess of blood and broken bits out onto the ground.

I hadn't realised how tightly I was squeezing William and Vincenzo's hands. William was clearly trying to hide his pain while Vincenzo seemed not to notice.

Klara was then turned away from us, her head leaned on a block. Her face looked out at us as her body turned to the side. Her eyes went to me for mere moments before she closed them.

Suren swung the axe. The thunk when it hit its target made me jump. Klara's eyelids fluttered and I thought I might vomit.

On the fourth swing there was a loud snap, and then a rush of blood as her head was finally separated from her neck.

I watched in shock as Suren lifted the head by the orange hair and showed it to the crowd, blood spattering all over her clothes and Gigi's precious stage.

"Justice is done!" Radu proclaimed.

"Why did they not say 'may God have mercy on your soul' before they began?" I asked no one in particular.

"It is believed that vampires have no soul," Vincenzo replied.

"She is really and truly gone. I cannot believe it." I could only sit and stare. We stayed seated as Les Vieux cleared themselves and the body from the stage.

"What will they do with her?" I asked.

"The body will be burned, the ashes scattered in two different places. That is part of the method. I thought I told you," Vincenzo said.

I smiled weakly. "You did. I am still recovering from the shock, that's all. I am sure you did not tell me the significance of the teeth smashing."

"Probably because I do not know it. It is merely part of the practice in different regions. I know the English do it, perhaps it is out of respect for Charles."

"It's barbaric," Morgana said angrily.

"You have never seen a Turkish execution." Sybilla pointed out.

Morgana chuckled. "And I pray I never will. I've seen enough for several lifetimes already."

Charles stood and readied himself to leave. We all followed him out row by row in an orderly fashion. William and I remained hand and hand as we walked outside.

"That is it? That's all?" I asked him quietly.

"She died with more dignity then she ever lived," William replied.

"I just cannot believe that after everything that has happened, it is all over in a moment. This time she is really gone, we saw it with our own eyes." I hesitated before saying, "I feel guilty that I am relieved."

He gently pat my hand. "Don't. She will have a much easier time in death than she ever had in life. Considering what she had done it was quite a simple death."

"Why, William, are you saying something nice about Klara?"

His face scrunched. "I do not speak ill of the dead, if I can avoid it."

When we got outside Prince Radu was talking with Sybilla, standing close to our carriage. The others were being loaded in to theirs; Gigi was staring angrily at us like she expected her gaze to have the power to kill. The rest of Les Vieux was speaking to Victorie as she was preparing to get into Charles's carriage.

"The two of you will be riding back without me," Vincenzo said when we approached him. "I have something I must attend to. I've had another carriage brought for you."

"Are you going to investigate that rumour?" I asked him.

He smiled. "Of course. Please present the idea to Morgana, see if she thinks its plausible. Ask her to keep it herself please."

"Of course. We look forward to your news," William said. He and I stood and watched Vincenzo leave before getting into our own carriage.

FURY

Prince Radu and Sybilla were privately dining in the conservatory that evening, and with the salon in full swing William and I were short on places where we could speak privately. I found the idea of dancing on the day Klara died a little unsettling so William and I went to the library.

"For the first time since this mess began I am relieved I don't have to be with Gigi," I said once we closed the door behind us.

William went to the hearth and began to build a fire. "You gave up your position for me."

He used a spell to ignite a flame once he had the logs in place then came to where I was standing by the window. He placed his hand on the small of my back, touching our shoulders together.

"She should not have forced me to choose," I said sharply, biting back tears. "She can cast me aside for whatever illogical reason she may have, but she cannot force me to choose."

"Thank you," he replied, his voice was soft and sweet. "We can leave now, if you so desire."

I could not help but laugh, a single tear falling from my cheek. "Charles and Vincenzo have done a lot for us both and we cannot take that for granted, my love. Not that the idea of leaving has not crossed my mind."

I heard the door open and close behind us, and Morgana said, "You two better not be plotting to leave me behind or I will hunt you down."

"I need to ask you something, Morgana, but you cannot repeat it to anyone other than us and Vincenzo," I replied, and we turned around to meet her.

Her face brightened as she smiled. "Are we running away?"

"Not yet," I continued. "But I want your opinion. Do you think it's possible to cure blood thirst?"

"What are you getting at?" Morgana snapped.

I rolled my eyes. "Just an opinion, Morgana."

She paused, watching my face closely before saying, "I suppose. Why? You would have to be quite powerful."

"Vincenzo heard a rumour, and we were wondering if there was any truth in it."

She looked at William. "You do not have an opinion?"

"My potion knowledge is limited." Was his response, and I wondered why I had not thought to ask.

"My opinion is that it could be done. But blood magic is very powerful and extremely dangerous. I would be cautious on many levels," Morgana said.

"That is why Vincenzo wants to keep this quiet. Charles would be running off so *he* was the first to have it, and that is unwise when we do not know what we are dealing with," William explained. There was a quick knock at the door and Hannah came in.

"Your presence is required in the salon," Hannah announced. "Signor Amori has returned and Les Vieux has arrived."

Before I could ask she added. "The request came from Lord Westwick. Specifically. For all of you."

"Thank you, Hannah," I said, smiling as we headed downstairs. She gave me a suspicious look as we walked past her.

The salon was quite lively, with Gigi at the centre of attention. Justice had been done, so there was no reason not to celebrate. I had to keep in mind as I looked around the room how many people Klara had slaughtered once she escaped captivity in the Holy Land. She had not just committed a crime against me.

Gigi watched me as I crossed the room and headed for Vincenzo. I wondered if she would ever stop tormenting me.

"Vincenzo told me what she said!" Charles's voice said quietly in my ear as he came up beside me. "Do not let her bother you. That is how she wins."

I smiled and nodded, and as he continued on ahead I saw Gigi coming close to me. Before I could do anything she slapped me hard across the mouth.

"Vous petite pute!" she spat at me. "You have betrayed me! How dare you shame me in public!"

She went to hit me again and I grabbed her arm. "Don't touch me."

My jaw ached when I spoke, she sneered at me and I wanted to poke her eyes out.

"I took you in and treated you like my own daughter! I should have left you where I found you!" she exclaimed loudly. I did not know what to do, she seemed to enjoy calling me out in public and I was already embarrassed. She was determined to humiliate me and I still did not know why.

Gigi came at me again and I grabbed her by the elbow and started pulling her to the back of the room. She slapped me again and I felt her fingernails scratch my face.

"You will regret not staying loyal to me for as long as you breathe!" she growled at me in a low voice.

"Finally! Some truth from you!" I exclaimed. "Maybe one more outburst and I will learn exactly what it is that's made you so angry."

She struck out at me again, this time wiggling out of my grasp.

"Screwing your way to the top is a vile way to live, you little whore! She was right all along, you are a rat!" Gigi yelled in my face. She was loud enough that people were stopping and turning.

"This coming from one of the great courtesans of France! How does that saying go? People in glass houses should *not throw stones!*" I hollered back. She gasped, and then turned to walk away.

"*I am not finished!*" I screamed, grabbing her arm and pulling her back. "Until tonight I genuinely cared about what I had done wrong, but *now*, after *this*...if you dare come at me like this again I swear on my family name I will tear you limb from limb!"

She smirked at me. "Your illegitimate name? Perhaps we should tell the world about your bastard mother and the Beast of Csejthe."

I could not stop my laughter. "And the bastard Valois, one in a long line of bastards for that matter, would be the authority on the subject wouldn't they?"

She lashed out again and I hit her closed fist in the face, grabbing her by the collar and pulling her up as she recoiled back.

"Not a word, do you understand me?" I said calmly in her ear, making sure my warm breath was on her neck. I shoved her back as hard as I could and she slammed into the wall with a crack. When she stood some dust fell, her shoulder having made a dent in the wall.

If she did not take me seriously now, I may actually have to try to kill her.

She stormed from the room in a blaze of pearls and skirts, the crowd parted to make way for her. I stayed in the back of the room as the waves of anger passed through me.

"You may never know why, Katrine." I was surprised when I turned to find Victorie standing behind me. "The thought is that the Delphine's who came *after* Gigi were insane, that it had skipped her somehow. But they were wrong."

"Should I try to do something?"

"No, you have done what was best. She knows now that she

cannot walk all over you, as she has done with many others. I hope you know you will have a life and succeed without her."

I smiled. "Thank you."

"Think nothing of it." She lightly touched my shoulder.

As she walked away I said, "Alienor is a lovely name."

"Some secrets are best kept hidden," she said without turning back.

WILLIAM'S ADVENTURE

"William asked me to invite you out with him for the day," Hannah said the next morning as she brought in my breakfast. "He reassured me it was nothing inappropriate but would be fun."

"Has Signor Amori returned?" I asked. She put the food tray down and began to busy herself picking out my clothes.

"Hannah?" I said her name; she jumped as if I'd startled her. "Has Vincenzo returned?"

"I have not seen him, and no one has mentioned him this morning," she replied without looking at me.

"Is something wrong?" I asked.

She pulled out one of my simple grey dresses and held it up in front of her so she could examine it. "No. Why?"

"No particular reason," I said, and I remained silent as she helped me get ready.

William was pacing around the front entryway as I came downstairs.

"Are you doing that because of me?" I asked him as Hannah helped me with my cloak.

"No," he replied.

"Then will you stop? You're making me nervous," I said quickly. He finally did, turning to smile happily at me when he noticed I was ready. He picked up a basket from its place beside the door, a servant tried to take it from him but he sent them away.

"Have you seen Vincenzo today?" I asked. He ignored me, stepping out and into our waiting carriage. It was a beautiful day with a warm breeze and the sun shining brightly, I pulled up my hood to try to cover my eyes.

"Why is everyone avoiding my questions about Vincenzo?" I said angrily as I sat down, William thumped on the roof of the carriage to get us moving.

"No one is avoiding. He has not returned, and it is not a big deal," he replied, before I could say anything he continued, "Sometimes he does this. He is very private about his feeding habits. You have no need to worry, he knows how to protect himself and he always comes back."

"And this is just accepted, no questions asked?"

"Tis a part of this life, my love. Now, are you excited for our adventure?"

"Is it possible to be excited for something I know nothing about?"

He frowned. "What about the surprise?"

"I suppose," I said, shrugging my shoulders.

We stepped out at the entrance to what appeared to be a stable.

"I do not understand," I said, watching him as he went on ahead of me with the basket.

"We're going to ride out and have a picnic," he said proudly.

"Ride out? You mean on a horse?"

"How else would we ride out?"

"You mean on the back of a horse? Why can't we just take the carriage?"

He chuckled. "You cannot take a carriage out to the middle of a field, Katrine."

I paused, considering what he was proposing. "Oh. Alright then."

"You do know how to ride a horse, don't you?" he asked. All I could do was stare blankly at him.

"How old are you?" he asked, shrugging me off before I could answer. "Never mind, I know that. How have you got this far in life without being able to ride?"

"To be honest, it's never come up. I suppose you could blame my parents, or Gigi," I said. "In fact, you could blame her for every one of my faults if you so wish."

He chuckled. "No time for that. You must learn to ride, but today you will ride with me."

I watched in awe as William and a stable boy prepared a beautiful light brown horse. It wasn't quite as large of an animal as the ones that pulled the carriages; but it was enough of one that it could kill a person if it kicked hard enough.

I knew it was silly to be afraid, being how common it was to ride. The animal was probably quite used to it and I assumed William had been riding since he could walk.

But my stomach still tightened as they approached the small bench I was seated at.

"A beautiful animal, don't you agree?" William said, patting the horse's neck and feeding it something out of his palm.

"And how exactly are we supposed to fit?" I asked.

"You have never seen two people ride together?"

"What about my skirts?"

"We will arrange them, do not worry. Now, it is time to go." He seemed quite proud of himself. The boy brought forward a small platform that William used to get up in the saddle and sit astride, then held out his hand for me.

He and William pulled me up so I had one leg on each side of the horses body, I adjusted my skirts as best I could but my shoes and ankles were exposed.

"Some may call it unseemly," I said.

"Until they make more appropriate riding gear so women don't have to ride side saddle if they prefer, 'some' may have to accept it. Now, hang on tightly to me." He directed my arms around him. I grabbed his waist and wrapped both arms around him, the horse sprung forward and we took off.

The way the air whips around when you are atop a horse makes you feel as if you are riding on the wind. It took some time for me to lift my head from where I had my cheek firmly pressed into his back, but when I did I felt like I was flying. Our bodies thumped up and down with the horse's movements, the countryside moving so quickly I had no chance to look.

But this did not seem to be about enjoying the view. It was about the bond between this majestic animal and its rider.

I gently kissed the back of William's neck, a tiny piece of skin that poked out from beneath his collar. I felt so close to him in that moment, clinging to his body while he was in control. I wanted to stay like this forever.

I was not sure I ever wanted to learn to ride on my own. This was far too enjoyable.

The horse began to slow as we approached a shaded area that had a view of lush green grass and beautiful landscape. He stopped the horse on a nice patch of green where it began to graze. He jumped down and walked us towards the tree, securing the reigns in such a way that the horse had room to walk around.

"So? Do you think you could do that on your own?" William asked. He reached out and grabbed my waist after I'd swung my leg over the horses body, holding me securely and helping me down while making sure I did not topple over.

"Why on earth would I do that?" I felt invigorated as my feet touched the ground. "I am not sure why any woman would if they get to be that close to the man they love."

He smiled. "I was hoping you would say that."

When my feet touched the ground we were standing so close the tips of our noses almost touched; he kissed me with an ease I had not felt from him before. He pulled away and our eyes stayed locked, the blue in his eyes seemed clearer than the sky.

"I brought a picnic," he said, proudly removing the saddle bag that I assumed contained whatever had been in that basket he'd been so clingy to.

"You planned all of this?" I asked. "I must admit I am quite impressed."

"I've been wanting to do this for a while but...," he paused for a moment, then said, "it was just not the right time."

"And I am sorry for that. If it seemed like I was being neglectful I did not mean to," I said.

He took my hand and led me to another clearing, where he lay out a blanket for us to sit in some shade but with a lovely view of the landscape.

"I had no idea there was such a beautiful countryside outside Paris." I was wide eyed trying to take in everything. "I do not know why anyone would live in the city."

"We could find a little cottage, leave all the nonsense behind."

I took his hand and squeezed it. "Not yet, my love."

He spread out some cold meat and cheese and began breaking up a roll of brown bread into chunks. I had not realised how hungry I was until I started to eat. He pulled out a bunch of red grapes and poured us mugs of mulled wine.

"You really have thought of everything," I said.

"Contrary to popular opinion I can be a sweet and romantic man," he replied. He paused, turning his head and staring off into a wooded area.

"Everything alright?" I asked. I tried to see what he was staring at, turning my eyes to the wooded area to see if there was anything suspicious.

I thought I saw something dark shift behind a tree, its shadow reflected on the grass.

"Yes," he said, turning back to me and smiling. "Now, let's enjoy our meal."

When we finished he cleared everything away and we lay back on the blanket. I stared up at the clear blue sky and the tops of the trees, the air seemed cleaner here somehow, breath moved easily through my body.

"William, may I ask you something?" I said, turning my head so I could look at him. "Do you have a family?"

"What do you mean?" he asked.

"Is your family alive? Do you speak with them? Where are they?"

He hesitated, and then said, "They are in Naples, and I do receive letters from them on occasion. I have six siblings, two brothers and four sisters. I am the youngest son."

"Do they all have magic like you?"

"If you're wondering if they all possess spell casting abilities, yes they do, but none of our magic is the same. My sister Bianca has the ability to manipulate the elements in a way none of the Santorini have ever possessed."

I smiled. "Santorini?"

He exhaled loudly. "Yes, my love. My family name is Santorini. Please keep it to yourself. We wouldn't want to ruin the image I have created for myself."

"Of course. We wouldn't want anyone to know you are really not a blue eyed demon." I could not help but laugh.

He smiled. "I am glad we understand each other."

I leaned over and softly kissed him on the cheek. "Thank you for sharing that with me."

"If we are to be together, even if you never meet them, there are things you should know. It's best for you not to be surprised by anything," he replied.

"I wish I could do the same for you, but sadly I know so little of the Bathory. And I am quite positive my father and brother are now just memories."

"We could go to Wallachia and see them."

I sighed and lay back, staring up at the sky. "Even if I wanted to, I could not go back without my mother. It is easier for all of us this way."

He slid his body over to we were touching side by side. He took my hand and held it over his chest. He squeezed my fingers, his body tensing as he turned back his attention to the wooded area.

"Do you think we will ever go to Naples?" I asked, trying to distract him. His lips moved only slightly and I felt the energy flow as he cast a spell.

"Naples is a dangerous place for witchcraft." William sat up quickly. His eyes remained turned and I started to get nervous.

"What's wrong?" I asked.

"Nothing."

"You would not cast a spell at 'nothing', William."

"Let me correct myself, it could be nothing. Perhaps we should move on."

I stared blankly at him, suddenly disappointed.

"I never said we would spend our whole day here. I have other things planned." He pulled me up with him. I stood and watched as he cleaned up and cast another spell over the area we had been in.

Before I could ask any questions we were back on the horse and on the move.

William took me on a tour of the countryside and small towns surrounding Paris. I was amazed at how pretty the areas were. They were nowhere near as rustic as back home and the places we had stopped in Hungary. The wars and constant fighting with the Turks had ravaged my homeland.

As we rode William seemed tense, and I developed the overwhelming feeling that we were being followed. We stopped and sat on an old stone wall that seemed to surround Paris to watch the sun set. The sky turned a reddish pink that blended into the clouds which were tinged with purple.

"Why can we not see this from the city?" I asked William.

"The buildings are in the way," he replied, taking my hand.

"I would not mind this life," I said. "I thought I would be really distraught at my life changing but, now, looking at this, I would not mind this."

"That is one reason I planned this, so you could see the world beyond *her* little bubble."

I chuckled. "She is very good at making you believe it is the greatest place, the only place one would ever care to be."

"It was one of her talents that made her a great courtesan. But now you are free, my love, to do as you please."

"What it pleases me to do are things that women do not traditionally do."

He smiled. "Perhaps it is time for the world to change."

He gently brushed a stray hair behind my ear and kissed me on the cheek.

"Courtesans are in the business of illusion and pleasure, it is about an experience. If that is all you are, it will envelope your whole life," he said. "Although she has been retired for some time and has this new profession it appears that all the great Grisela Delphine is, is a courtesan."

"It is hard not to be something when it's all you've ever known, and your mother and grandmother before you," I explained. "That is why I've always wanted more for my life. I did not want to be so easily defined. I did not want to be just somebody's wife and mother."

"I believe that marriage should be about partnership," he said.

"Is that what your parents were like?"

He chuckled. "My mother is a force of nature. You could not

be anything other than her partner. Not that my father isn't a force of his own. I have never met two people who love each other in such a way."

"I would love to meet them. Your siblings as well."

"Maybe one day," he said softly. "Are you cold? We could go back, if you wish."

I leaned my head on his shoulder. "Let's stay a while. We may not have an opportunity like this again."

THIN AIR

When I woke the next morning the ray of sunlight that shone in the window was the most beautiful thing, and made me so happy I could not stop smiling. The world seemed like a more amazing place, and I could not help but focus on everything good and wonderful in this world.

Hannah watched me peculiarly when she brought my breakfast.

"You are awfully sunny this morning," Hannah said as she put down the tray and I dug right in.

"Is is a crime to be happy?" I asked. "William took me on a wonderful outing yesterday. And do not worry, my maidenhood is fully intact."

"I am so happy for you, Katrine. You truly deserve some joy after all you've been through. Now, Signor Amori has resurfaced and he'd like to meet with you."

"Have you seen William yet today?"

"No," she replied. "Now, we need to get you dressed. Signor Amori said you could bring your breakfast if you're not finished."

I walked passed William's closed door on my way to Vincenzo's room, and something did not seem right.

Vincenzo opened his door and looked surprised. "Where's William?"

I turned and knocked on William's door, and when I got no answer I opened it and Vincenzo and I stepped inside.

The room was empty, and looked as if William had been gone for days.

"Something does not seem right," Vincenzo said flatly as he walked the room.

"Hannah!" I called out and her face appeared in the doorway. "Find out where William is. Please."

She nodded and left, I turned my attention back to Vincenzo.

"He was strange yesterday. He kept looking around like he was seeing something I wasn't, and he was casting spells when we'd leave a place like he was covering our tracks." I moved things around and examined objects in the room looking for a clue.

"Did you notice anything?" he asked.

"I thought I sensed someone following us, but I can't be sure," I replied. "Why?"

"This seems strange. Can you not feel that?"

I stood silently for a moment, and then said, "There is a strange....something in the air. I can't put my finger on it."

"No one has seen him since you two returned last night, Mademoiselle," Hannah said, her face appearing in the doorway.

"It's not like him to just disappear," Vincenzo told me.

"Exactly," I replied, and then said to Hannah. "Call Lord Westwick and the others and ask them to come to the library."

She nodded and left without needing an explanation.

"What do you think could have happened to him?" My emotions began to swirl and my voice started to tremble.

"Someone either wanted him enough to take him or wanted him gone. I do not think he just *left*." Vincenzo's tone was very abrupt. He clearly sensed something I did not.

"Who would want him gone?" I asked him. Before he could reply I stormed out and headed for the library.

Gigi stood beside Charles with a stupid smirk on her face that made my anger boil over. I reached out my hand, without a word of a spell she flew across the room into my grip and I tightened my hands around her throat.

"You did something to him, didn't you?" I growled at her. I heard Vincenzo explaining the situation to the others. "You would go to such great lengths to hurt me? You are sick!"

"Even if I wanted to, and believe me I've thought about it, do you really think I am powerful enough to hurt him?" Gigi sputtered as I continued to squeeze. "I am a dhampir. I do not have that kind of power."

"So maybe you brought in some help! I don't believe you are strong enough alone but if you had some assistance." I was so angry I thought I might explode. "I swear on everything that is Holy that if you had any part in his disappearance I will kill you myself."

Vincenzo took a hold of one of my arms and pulled me off of her. "She gets the point, Katrine."

"He's just gone, you say?" Charles asked.

"Into thin air," Vincenzo said.

Gigi chuckled. "Maybe he smartened up and left you."

I slapped her so hard she stumbled, the red hand print on her cheek growing dark. Vincenzo put his body in between us.

"Did you notice anything strange?" Charles stood beside Vincenzo. Natalia had wandered away to look at the books, Sybilla and Morgana watched me anxiously from the couch while Prince Radu stood by the fireplace.

"There was a residual something in his room, and Katrine said he was acting peculiar when they were out yesterday," Vincenzo said as my gaze shifted back and forth between Sybilla and Prince Radu. Sybilla just shrugged her shoulders while

Morgana up and left.

"This *is* odd," Charles replied.

"So what are we going to do about this?" I asked to no one in particular.

"We must discover the cause before we can plan a solution," Charles said.

"Someone took him," Morgana said sharply as she returned and sat back down. My eyes moved to Gigi.

"Kidnapping William of Naples would be no easy task, especially in a house full of people. Whoever did it is not only very powerful but very serious," she continued, turning to me and pointing at Gigi. *"She is not capable, there is no question. "*

"Pardon me for intruding, but may I say something?" Prince Radu asked. I motioned for him to continue. "It has been in my experience that only witch hunters are capable of something this elaborate."

"What do you mean 'elaborate'?" I asked.

"To remove a being such as William from a full house would be complex and involve a considerable amount of power. It would take some thought and effort, something that witch hunters are trained to do," Prince Radu explained. "And with the boy being from Naples and a prominent magical family, it would be easy to assume that the Cesari are responsible."

Charles and Vincenzo froze, they looked like frightened animals.

"One of you better start explaining why you look so frightened or I swear to my Lord in Heaven....," I started, my voice rising in anger.

Charles sighed; he and Vincenzo stared at each other, like they were speaking through their gaze.

"William said he left Naples because of the Cesari," Vincenzo said. "They'd been killing his family for hundreds of years and he believed it was his best chance at survival. I am ashamed to say I have forgotten everything else he said."

"So how do we find them?" I asked. It seemed like the whole room paused and my anger began to overflow.

"Why are you all just standing there? If a plan is needed, then let's make one!" I said loudly, and then I turned to Prince Radu. "How do I find them?"

"I am afraid it is not that simple," he replied.

"It would be easier if we just left him to die." When no one replied I gasped.

"Fine. Fine. That is perfectly fine," I said, backing out of the room. "If you will not help me I will do it myself. I cannot believe you would abandon him like this."

"Katrine, please. We are not abandoning him! But we are not strong enough to take them on!" Vincenzo replied, his tone trying to be soothing.

"Can Les Vieux not intervene?" I asked Prince Radu, and by his expression I knew that I would not get the answer I needed.

I turned and ran from the room. I could not look at them for another second.

I slammed the basement door behind me and clattered down the stairs, my vision blurred by unshed tears.

"Who's there?" Gabriel called out in the darkness. I ran back to his cell and pushed open the door, and fell into a heap on the floor and began to sob.

"Katrine? What has happened?" he rushed to me, sat down and pulled me into his arms.

"William," I stuttered. "Witch hunters have kidnapped William."

"Did you tell Charles? What is the..."

"They will do nothing! But I can't let him die. I will have to go on my own."

"You will do no such thing! I will help you with whatever you need, cousin."

I hugged him tightly. "I knew I could count on you."

"But you must understand that I will have to ask my contacts for help. Are you comfortable with that?"

"Whatever it takes. I will speak with Countess Zrinyi myself, if needed."

"Great. So we shall leave at sundown."

"Cousin, may I stay here with you until then? I cannot bear to face them on my own." I began to sob.

He stroked my hair as he held me close to him. "Do not worry, my sweet. I am here for you."

FAMILY COMFORT

I cried until I fell asleep on the dirt floor, curled up like a small child in Gabriel's arms. I felt safe and a comfort I had never felt from a human being since my Mother. Even his smell was soothing.

When I opened my eyes and I realised that he had not moved, had not even shifted me an inch. I was overwhelmed with a feeling that I did not recognise.

A thought came into my mind and it pulled everything together.

Only your true family could bring you such comfort.

"Are you alright, child?" he asked, his voice cutting through my thoughts.

"Thank you, cousin, for staying with me," I said. I pulled away from him and we stayed sitting together on the ground. Something about the coldness centred me.

"It is my pleasure. You would be quite surprised at how many Bathory women have come to me when they needed to cry." He smiled and looked away, lost in his memories. "I need to ask you how you know for sure that William was taken by witch hunters."

"Prince Radu suggested it, and the others did not argue. Morgana said she believed it was something powerful, and Vincenzo said William had mentioned them," I replied. "He called them Cesari."

Gabriel hesitated. "Well, that does make things more complicated."

"Not you too!" I exclaimed. Before I could do anything else he took my face between his hands.

"Listen to me closely." He kept his eyes locked on mine. "It does not mean I will not help you but you must know what you are up against. The Cesari are one of the oldest and strongest families of witch hunters on the continent; they are responsible for killing more than half of the magical families in the Italian territories."

"Is there no hope?"

He smiled. "There is always hope. But this will not be simple. And we will need help."

I kept my eyes locked on him. "Whatever it takes."

After I had straightened myself and dusted the dirt from my dress Gabriel and I went upstairs.

Hannah was sitting on a stool close to the door, as if she was waiting for me.

"Can you fix us some food?" I asked her. She stared at me silently for a moment, and then motioned to two stools by the counter where we could sit and wait.

"Should I change my dress?" I asked Gabriel. My dress was plain grey but well made, nice but not extravagant.

"No. You're there to talk, not attract attention," Gabriel replied. Hannah handed us our plates, I hadn't realised I was so hungry.

I heard the entrance from the dining room open and close, someone came quietly up behind us.

"Shall this kill me?" I asked without turning around. "Have you seen something I should know about?"

I turned to face Morgana. "Did you know this was coming? Do you hate him so much that you would simply allow this to happen?"

"I saw nothing, and I do not hate him," Morgana said flatly. "I cannot allow you to go after him alone."

"Well, no need to trouble yourself because my cousin and I will deal with the situation. Besides, it seems you much prefer to cower in fear with the others."

"I was in shock!" she yelled. "You cannot judge me on that!"

I paused, surprised by the forcefulness of her tone. I had never seen her behave in such a manner.

I turned to Gabriel. "Would her presence disturb any of our plans?"

"No," he replied, shrugging his shoulders. "But she cannot tell the others."

"Splendid. Now, go and get yourself prepared. We shall leave before people being to arrive for the salon," I told her. Morgana nodded and Hannah moved into her place as she left.

"Begging your pardon, Mademoiselle, but may I speak freely?" Hannah asked, before I could reply she continued. "Is this safe? Perhaps if you speak with Signor Amori and..."

"I have spoken with them already, and if I wait for them to decide William will be dead," I said sharply. "My cousin and I can take care of this. You have no need to worry."

Hannah's lips squeezed together tightly as she stopped herself from speaking, if she had a chance to get me alone I would surely never hear the end of it.

She simply nodded and returned to her duties.

"She has little faith in me," Gabriel said quietly.

"She does not know you, and has known Vincenzo for most of her life," I replied. "She is simply concerned. A lot has happened that would give her cause to do so."

"So I can assume you questioned Gigi?"

"The only thing they were confident of was the fact that she does not have the power to pull this off, even with help."

"Could they all be..."

"No. Vincenzo would never....no. I am confident this is outsiders."

He took another sip of his wine. "And the Scots girl?"

"We could use the assistance. She has some magic," I replied.

"If you are finished, we should get moving," he said. I asked one of the servants to fetch Morgana as we headed out to the front entryway.

Luckily no one was around, but I caught a glimpse of Vincenzo at the top of the stairs as we went out the door.

Morgana was right; I could not judge someone for their shock and fear. But I did not have the option of waiting until they came to their senses.

"May I ask where we are going?" Morgana asked once the carriage was moving.

"We are going to speak with my contacts to see if they can be of any assistance," Gabriel said. Morgana's eyes shifted to me for mere seconds.

"You may get to meet Countess Zrinyi," I added.

"Oh. How lovely." Morgana gave me a confused look. I smiled, trying to reassure her by my expression that I knew exactly what I was doing.

Gabriel took my hand. "Your fidgeting is a clear sign of nervousness."

"What if they refuse to help as well?" I asked.

"No one *refused*, Katrine," Morgana said angrily.

"They *stood* there like a bunch of imbeciles! It was like they did not even care!" My voice rose in anger. "They use him to frighten people then do nothing when he is in danger! How much has he done to protect *them* and when it comes down to it they desert him! Of course they would not help *the blue eyed demon*."

I stopped myself from continuing and tried to focus on my breathing. My companions sat silently, Gabriel still with a firm grip on my hand.

When the carriage stopped my heart jumped into my throat, the realisation of how complicated my life had become was sinking in.

"You have not changed your mind?" Gabriel asked.

"I need to get him back, cousin," I said. He nodded and we silently stepped out into the night.

I was shocked at the large country house that stood before me. It was probably one of the biggest homes I had ever seen.

The large wood door opened and a figure stepped into the threshold, the light from behind making the person unrecognizable. But they appeared to nod at Gabriel, stepping away as a sign for us to enter.

Countess Zrinyi was standing by an enormous fireplace as we entered. I had a sudden flash of a similar moment in Castle Csejthe, my fingers going immediately to my Grandmother's ring.

"Cousin, I am most pleased to see you," Countess Zrinyi said.

"I wish I had come under better circumstances, Anna. But we need help. The Order's help." Gabriel stood tall as he spoke, and I got a glimpse of the commander he once was. "My cousin's intended, a sorcerer named William of Naples, has been taken by witch hunters. We need to get him back."

She raised an eyebrow. "And why on earth would we want to do that?

"Please, Anna. Show some compassion. And, as a member of the Order I have every right to ask," Gabriel replied.

"He is right, Anna," a man said, stepping into the room from the shadows. "Regardless of your personal prejudices, Gabor is still one of us."

"Thank you, Ivan. It is good to see you, my friend," Gabriel said. "May I present Katrine and Morgana."

He chuckled as we both bowed. "She is everything they have

spoken of. It is an honour to finally meet you, Katrine, and you as well, young druid."

"Have you heard anything about the kidnapping?" Gabriel asked Ivan. The man said nothing.

"It was the Cesari, wasn't it?" Gabriel asked Ivan who nodded in agreement. "Is the boy already dead?"

"No. It will not be easy to retrieve him. The Cesari are not exactly known for negotiations," Ivan replied.

"That is irrelevant," I said quietly. "He is coming with us, whether they like it or not."

Ivan smiled. "Spoken like a true Bathory. I suppose that means you will also use whatever means necessary to do so?"

"Yes, my lord," I replied.

"I am not sure it is wise for us to get involved," Countess Zrinyi said. "It could turn into a political nightmare for us."

"One of your members, a woman, approached me on several occasions. Where is she? May I speak with her?" I asked.

"Why?" Ivan's eyes were a bright shade of blue.

"Because perhaps someone who was so eager to help me before would be more receptive to doing so now."

Ivan's head tilted slightly. "I never said we would not help."

"But you do not sound interested in doing so. Do not worry, you would not be the first," my tone was flippant and full of anger, "and I am not at the point where I am willing to beg. But I will get William back, regardless of whether I need to do it alone."

Ivan turned to Countess Zrinyi, who looked extremely annoyed. I thought about pleading with her but it seemed silly. Looking pathetic in front of her would not help the situation.

"The Order will help you retrieve William of Naples from the Cesari, Katrine Bathory," Ivan said when he turned back to me. "Come back tomorrow and we shall begin."

"Tomorrow!" I exclaimed. "But he could be dead by then!"

"He won't be," Countess Zrinyi said, and then she left the room without another word.

"Tomorrow," Ivan said, bowing to us and leaving himself. Gabriel took my arm and led us back out to our carriage.

The chateau was all a buzz when we returned. Hannah was waiting in the entry hall for us.

"There is a woman here to see you," Hannah said as she took off my cloak. "She is in the salon with Lord Westwick."

"Does this woman have a name?" I asked.

"All I know is that she speaks Italian," Hannah said, and then she disappeared into the house.

Gabriel, Morgana and I went together into the salon. They stayed close to me as I approached Charles and the woman he spoke to. She had blonde hair the colour of wheat and was dressed in beautiful green silk; the slightly different cut I assumed was popular in Italy. When she turned to me I was immediately drawn to her stunning blue eyes.

"Here is Mademoiselle Bathory," Charles said.

"Lovely!" the woman began. "I am Bianca di Napoli, and I am looking for my brother."

Charles's mouth gaped open. "Your brother?"

"Yes, my brother. You're William of Naples," she replied. I stood and stared, my only thought was that I was shocked she was not only speaking Italian.

"It is a pleasure to finally meet you," Bianca said to me. "I assume you are returning from looking for my brother? They took him, did they not?"

"Yes, they did. And yes, I am. I will do whatever is necessary to bring him back, Signorina," I said, biting back tears.

"Please! You are to be my sister, you must call me Bianca," she replied, pulling me into her arms and embracing me warmly. "You are la mia famiglia."

"I am so pleased to see you," I said, the smell of fresh lavender and rain perfuming her. "And please, call me Katrine. Let me introduce you to the others."

CHANGE OF CIRCUMSTANCES

She slept in his room. She insisted upon it. The others were so in shock that I had to take care of everything, luckily Hannah was ready and willing to help.

We brought Bianca breakfast together; she was already up and dressed when we came to the door.

"Good morning, ladies," Bianca said as Hannah placed the tray on the table he took his meals at.

"Good morning, Bianca. This is my maid, Hannah. If you should need anything she is at your disposal," I said. We sat at the table; I dismissed Hannah so we could speak in private. "I must ask, not that I am not pleased to see you, but how did you know he was gone?"

"I have been tracking the Cesari," she started. "And they do not often dispatch all of their strongest when on a mission, unless they are going to collect someone particularly strong. When I heard they had sent such a group to Paris I could only assume it was for William. When I saw your face last night I knew for sure it was true. He left Naples to try to escape this life, and so far had achieved it. But he must have done something to attract their attention. Do you know what that could have been?"

I sighed. "I am afraid not. There was one thing while we were in Russia but that was over a year ago."

"Perhaps it is his connection to this group. What are you doing to find him?"

"The group is too frightened to do anything, my cousin and I have been in contact with the Order of the Dragon and they have agreed to help."

She raised an eyebrow. "You have the ear of the Order?"

"My cousin does. Help is needed and they are willing. We shall go see them tonight when my cousin rises."

"He is a vampire, your cousin?"

"Yes, so we must work at night."

"The others are too frightened? Do you think your former mentor has anything to do with this?"

I felt my face flush with embarrassment. "He told you?"

"You gave up your life for him, Katrine. He has never known such love. He sent me a letter for some sisterly advice on how to handle himself. His experience with honest women is minimal."

"I could not bear it if I lost him."

She took my hand in hers, her skin was warm and it spread through up my arms and into my body.

"You will *not, we will not* lose him. My parents lost their siblings and I will *not lose mine*. Do you understand?" Bianca said forcefully. "I will burn Paris to the ground first."

I smiled and squeezed her hand. "I am glad we are on the same page."

"I apologise for my forcefulness. As I am sure you know, our family is hot blooded."

I laughed. "Yes, your brother is not very good at controlling his hot blood. It should be interesting formally introducing you to the others....well, those you can meet while the sun is shining."

"I thought I met them yesterday," she said as she finished

her food.

"You did, but things have to be done a bit more formally because you will be staying. Normally it would fall to William, but perhaps it is better that it falls to me," I replied. "And, I must tell you now, in accordance with William's wishes I will introduce you as Bianca di Napoli."

"Do you think he is ashamed?"

"No, I believe he wants to keep his private life private."

She squeezed my hand. "That's fine. Let us do what we need to do, and then we can get to finding William."

The others had gathered in the conservatory for a meal, and as a way for me to introduce Bianca to the group. She wore darker green, I wondered if it was her signature colour.

"You have the loveliest taste," I said as we headed downstairs. "Your gowns are exquisite."

"Thank you, I design them myself and my sisters and I make them together. We have quite the little business," she replied.

"That's fantastic. Perhaps we can create something together one day. I love doing embroidery," I said. "I hope you will have the chance to meet our costumer."

Before she could say more we were in the room, she took my arm as I began to make the introductions.

Bianca smiled happily as Vincenzo kissed her knuckles. "It is an honour to finally meet you, Signor Amori. My brother has told me great things."

"We are so pleased to have you, Signorina. I wish it was under better circumstances," he said, and Bianca's smile faded.

"What are you doing to change that, Signor?" Bianca asked, and then moved on before he could say more.

"Ah, Lord Westwick," Bianca began as we came to Charles. "And what are you doing to ensure the safety of your other members, now that your muscle is gone?"

I could not help but smile at her ability to say all the things that I could not.

"And this is Morgana, she will be helping us this evening," I said. Bianca and Morgana shook hands; the two seemed quite pleased with each other.

"I have never met a druid before," Bianca said.

Morgana smiled. "I sincerely hope I can be of some help."

"This is Victorie de la Reina," I said, she and Bianca also shook hands. Bianca looked startled when their skin touched, staring into Victorie's face without saying a word.

"And this is Grisela Delphine," I said flatly, she had taken the last place in the line. Gigi smiled an evil look that made my skin crawl. The two women touched hands for a mere second and Gigi's face went as white as a sheet. I tried to hide my smile, the prospect of Bianca scaring Gigi made me almost giddy.

"Lovely to meet you, Signorina di Napoli," Gigi said, her voice a bit squeaky.

"Lovely to meet you as well," Bianca said as Gigi hurried out of the room.

"Should I ask?" I whispered to her.

"No. We should enjoy our meal and prepare for the evening ahead."

I was shocked and appalled at the behaviour of the others; they ate and said nothing, they were so petrified of Bianca's wrath. The only joy was watching how amused Morgana was by the entire situation.

"They are all very afraid of my brother," Bianca said quietly to me.

"Morgana sometimes calls him 'the blue eyed demon'." I chuckled. "But that is all in good fun. Now, they have a great respect for each other."

She raised an eyebrow. "Now?"

"'Tis a long story. But she is true to her word and she will do what she can to help us."

"So now we wait on your cousin?" Bianca asked.

"Yes, unfortunately the sun is against us."

I realised when Bianca laid eyes on Gabriel for the first time that we had more than the sun against us.

It was not Gabriel's fault that he was attractive, nor was it Bianca's fault for having womanly desires. But I sincerely hoped that such things would not hinder us.

"Cousin, this is William's sister, Bianca di Napoli. She has come to help us," I said, Bianca extended her hand and he softly kissed her knuckles. "Bianca, this is Gabriel Bathory."

"I apologise for keeping you waiting because of my circumstances," he said.

"It is no problem, Monsieur Bathory. I am most sincerely glad for your help," Bianca replied. "I heard you have the ear of the Order, are they willing to help us?"

He chuckled. "I do not know about willing but they have agreed to, which is enough."

She snorted. "Better than the members of this company. I am quite appalled; as I am sure you can imagine a loving sister would be."

"Yes, it saddens me to think of how my own sister was affected by my death," he replied. He extended his arm to her and I followed behind as they walked the salon together.

Vincenzo approached me silently; I continued walking without saying a word to him. He handed me something wrapped up in fabric.

"I know you are angry," he said quietly. "And I am ashamed to say I am afraid. I hope you can forgive me, and giving you this is really all the good I can do."

I unwrapped the fabric and found a dagger in its sheath, a red stone imbedded into the end of the handle.

"It does at your ankle," he continued. "It belonged to the one who turned me, and I used it to...hopefully it will bring you some luck."

"Thank you, mon ami," I replied.

"I hope you will not judge me too harshly for being afraid."

"As long as you come looking for us if we do not return," I said.

He stopped me, pulling me into his embrace and kissing my cheeks.

"I will raise an army, I swear it. And if what you are doing does not work, come home and we will regroup and make a new plan. I will not desert you, I promise," he said in my ear. I hugged him tightly, my fears and anxiety washing though me as if he was somehow pulling them out of my body.

"I have to go," I said, pulling away from him. He nodded, and I quickly headed for the door before I could start to cry.

SHADOWS

Bianca taught me how to strap the dagger sheath to my calf; she had something similar strapped to her own leg.

Its weight gave me a sense of security that I found odd, since I had never handled a knife before.

Ivan looked startled when we stepped into the main room of the Order's residence. Countess Zrinyi was again by the fire.

"Signorina di Napoli, we are honoured by your presence," Ivan said, bowing politely to her.

"I am honoured that you have agreed to help find my brother. My family is in your debt, sir," Bianca replied.

My heart sank. I had not thought of what the Order would want in return for their help, but if it did not bother Bianca I would not dwell on it.

"Please call me Ivan," he said. "And this is Countess Zrinyi. She will be helping us on this excursion."

"Thank you, Countess Zrinyi. I cannot express how much I appreciate your assistance." I had to fight back tears.

"I am not doing this for you, child," she said sharply. "I am doing this for my cousin."

Gabriel smiled. "Thank you, Anna."

"My hope is that you will see the error in your ways and decide to join us," she added. The eagerness in her voice was heartbreaking.

"Enough with the pleasantries, let us prepare for the task at hand." Ivan clapped his hands to call our attention. "The Cesari are hiding in a cottage in the woods outside Paris. It is not an ideal situation since they can use the woods to their advantage. Our information says there are six of them, and they are being led by a young woman called Colombina."

"I've heard of her," Bianca said. "She has killed three of my cousins. She's been after my sister Gemma. They have come to blows more than once."

"It seems as if she is trying to establish a name for herself within the Cesari. I have heard that she has a reputation for torture," Ivan continued, turning to me when I gasped. "You must prepare yourself for the eventuality that he is hurt. And the more he fights back the worse it will get."

My chest began to ache. I grabbed Gabriel's arm for support.

"We will have to approach on foot, under the cover of darkness. You will have to leave the carriage at quite a distance and use magic to conceal your path," Ivan said to us, then focused on Morgana. "It'll have to be your magic, druid. The Cesari will sense if Signorina di Napoli uses hers."

Morgana nodded. "Of course. That is what I had expected."

"Are you prepared to kill them on sight?" he asked. "You will have no choice for they will be trying to do the same."

We all nodded collectively. I knew this would be no easy task, and I wondered if it was, in fact, better that the others were not included.

The members of the Order that came with us rode out on horseback, including Countess Zrinyi. It reminded me of that last day with William and I wanted to cry, but now was not the time to show any weakness.

Bianca and Gabriel were equally stoic, like they were marching into battle. Only Morgana reached out and we held hands as we rode, the carriage getting rough once we left the city.

I could not focus on my fear, only the task at hand. If anything happened to William I would never forgive myself.

Stepping out into the darkness all I could see what the movement of large, dark figures; the members of the Order sat atop enormous black chargers. They reminded me of the horses from the witch's carriage, the image of Darvulia so fresh in my mind it made me cringe. I looked out into the darkness of the forest; I could not imagine how we could find anything in that.

"Do not forget that you are a daughter of the darkness, Katrine," Morgana said quietly. "You can use it to your advantage."

"It's just so overwhelming." My eyes remained on the forest. Only then did I notice that she was casting a spell on the carriage, I assumed to conceal it.

"We will spread out through the forest," Ivan's said, I could not tell which figure was him. "Gabor knows what to do. I would suggest you all stay together. It will be safer."

Without another word, the four dark figures were off their horses and moving into the forest, soon they blended in like shadows and I lost sight of them completely.

"Let's move, I do not want them too far ahead," Gabriel said, and we started our silent trudge into the forest.

Navigating through the trees was easier than I had expected, it reminded me of my village and I felt oddly comfortable.

"Can you sense anything? Are we getting close?" Morgana asked me, her hand still clutched in mine. I pushed out my senses and they slammed into something like a brick wall in the middle of the trees.

"There is something, but I am not sure if it is them," I replied. "But we will move in that direction."

"Can you sense William?" Bianca asked.

I paused. "No. But there is something else, perhaps their only animals."

We kept on in the direction of the magical wall, which I assumed was the protection around the house. It was so big and so strong I was surprised the others could not feel it.

The Order had all but disappeared. I had to struggle to sense them and it would only last a few seconds. I hoped that meant they were doing what they said they would.

And there was something else, like a soft breeze on my senses. Something else was with us, and I could not place what it was.

As we got closer to the wall it began to feel like a weight on my shoulders.

"That's quite a defence they've put up," Morgana said as we continued to get closer.

"We'll have to knock it down." Bianca's voice was flat and empty. We approached the wall, close enough that the weight began to suffocate me. I had to stop and there was still no sign of the house.

Bianca raised her hand as if she was going to cast, Morgana put out an arm to stop her.

"Not yet," Morgana said. She picked up a stick off the group and threw it forward, it bounced and sent a splinter of electricity up and around the point of contact.

"Maria Madre di Dio," Bianca said as she stared ahead of us. A string of obscenities in rapid Italian quickly followed, so quickly that I questioned whether she was casting a spell or not.

But spells did not include curse words, to the best of my knowledge.

"I cannot see the house," Gabriel said.

"That is probably part of the cover spell," Morgana continued. "As soon as we use magic they will know we are here."

There was a loud snap from in the distance that made us jump, the wall shook with little snaps of electricity.

"Does anyone see the irony in witch hunters using such powerful magic?" Morgana asked.

"The others are attacking the wall," Gabriel said. "You may strike when ready, but prepare yourself."

Bianca smiled, and she began to slowly turn her wrist. A coil of fire wound out of her hand until she was holding what looked like a whip made of crackling flames.

"I like her already," Morgana mumbled. She raised her hands. A ripple began moving up the wall from the ground.

Bianca began whipping the wall as one would whip a prisoner, leaving long lashes of fire that I thought may drip with blood.

Gabriel grabbed my arm. "Be ready. We do not know what lies beyond."

I nodded and tried to concentrate on the hole that Bianca was creating. Another snap ripped through the silence, and Bianca's lashes became a human sized hole.

"Hurry!" I yelled, grabbing Bianca and pulling Gabriel along as I charged to the hole.

Somehow he got away from me, lagging behind as Bianca and I tumbled into the hole and it closed behind us.

It was as if we were standing alone in the dark forest; no sounds, no sight or sign of Morgana or Gabriel.

I stared at where the hole had been in utter confusion.

"Come on, Katrine! We have to go!" Bianca said as she tried to pull me away.

"But...," I struggled with words.

"They will have sensed the tear, they will be coming! We have to go!" she said, pulling hard until I followed her into the forest.

THE FALL

"Bianca! Bianca! We can't just go on! We *need* them!" I called to her as she ran ahead of me. The more she ran, the farther away we would get from the wall, and the others.

"I told you, we have to put distance between us and the hole! They'll know what we've done and send people to kill us," she said angrily. "And I will not die in the forest like a common animal."

We continued on in silence and I used my senses to try to keep an idea of where we were. Bianca suddenly felt strange. The wall became overwhelming again with the flicker of something else on the edge of my senses.

Those flickers began to get closer, and I gasped when I felt them breach the wall.

Bianca stopped suddenly, as if she felt it too, and then continued on.

I lumbered along behind her, suddenly feeling large and awkward. I got no clear sense of anything as to where the house may be.

I thought to say something, but decided to act as if I was out of breath. We could only run so far, we were in their territory after all.

I stopped, hunched over and tried to level my breathing as if I was trying to catch my breath.

"What is wrong?" Bianca asked.

"Should we not be looking for the house? Especially if the others cannot get through? We are his only hope," I asked, standing and righting myself once I steadied my breathing.

She paused. "Of course. I thought I saw something up ahead. Let's keep moving."

There was nothing ahead. I could not even tell if we were close to the wall; I could sense the wall was there but had lost all the idea of direction.

"Can you not sense anything? Feel their magic?" I asked as we slowed.

She gave me a sideways glance without stopping. "Can you?"

A cloaked figured came out of the darkness ahead of us, I braced myself for a magical attack.

Pushing the hood back, Countess Zrinyi's face was as clear as if she was shining light from her body.

"How did you get through?" I asked.

She came closer to me and stood between Bianca and I. "Ivan pushed me through so I could find you."

"Why only you? What's going on?" I asked. She withdrew a sword from her belt and charged at Bianca.

All I could do was scream as Countess Zrinyi drove her sword in Bianca's gut all the way to the hilt.

I tried to lunge for Bianca but the Countess pushed me off.

"What have you done?" I shrieked as blood began to pour from Bianca's mouth.

"You have been fooled, child," Countess Zrinyi said. She pulled out her sword, and as Bianca's body fell to the ground she changed into a black haired woman dressed in men's clothes.

"When you went through the wall Bianca did not get through. One of the Cesari was waiting on the other side and took on her face so she could mislead you." She put her hand on my shoulder. "Do not worry, Bianca is out on the other side with Gabor and your druid. And I must say she is not pleased."

"Thank you for coming to my aid. I do not know what to say," I said quietly. "How do we get them through?"

She paused for a moment. "I am not sure we can."

"But how can we find the house? I have been wandering the forest and..."

She pointed at the body at our feet. "*That* is why you have found nothing. I am sure of it. We must continue on, and if the others can get through they will soon follow."

I could not help but stare at the body as the stomach wound continued to bleed. "It all happened to fast. How would I have known if you had not come along?"

"You wouldn't have," she said flatly. "She had probably planned to lead you around the forest until she grew weary then killed you. Or something worse, I do not have any experience with witch hunters. I am only going with what Ivan said."

"What is he like as a man, this Ivan?" I asked as we continued farther into the forest.

"Why do you ask?"

"My cou...Gabriel, I mean Gabor, seems to respect this man, and I would like to know more about him. I know very little of Gabor's life that does not directly involve me."

She smiled. "Ivan is a good, fair, and honest man. He is worthy of whatever respect my cousin has for him."

"Gabor is worried that the Bathory are being recruited."

"He knows that many of our family have been called by the Order," she paused for a moment. "Please tell him that he and I are the only ones that I am aware of, in this case. There is great interest in you and your Mother."

"May I ask why?" I said, and then quickly wished I hadn't.

"It is something about your Mother's father. They do not say much in my presence, for they fear they would insult me."

"Did you ask why they did not get *her* from her prison?"

She paused at the mention of her Mother. "Every day for the first month I was with them. I never got a straight answer, but she had been gone from this earth for a year by that point."

I rushed to catch up with her so we were walking at the same pace. "It is a true testament to the content of your character that you did not murder me."

She continued on and said nothing. I did not push. I only wanted her to know that I understood, in my own way, how hard my existence must be for her, and to thank her for allowing me to continue to on.

I grabbed her arm the instant I saw lights up ahead. We stood and watched in silence as I tried to focus my eyes in the darkness and see where the lights were coming from.

I spread out my senses, and the lights were clearly coming from windows once I was able to centre myself. The feeling of William became overwhelming, as if he were a lighthouse sending out a beam to guide us.

Before I could speak those flickers on the outside of my senses became something more solid.

"How many?" Countess Zrinyi asked.

"Pardon?" I replied.

"In the house? How many?"

"Five, and William," I said. I turned my eyes only slightly, catching a flicker of something white out of the corner of my eye.

When I turned my head a white wolf stepped further into a clearing. Countess Zrinyi stepped back when she saw her, preparing to run.

"It's okay," I said. "They're with me."

"They're from your group?" she asked.

"Yes. And they walked right through the barrier. I guess the Cesari did not prepare for shapeshifters," I replied. I smiled as I sensed that Charles and the other shifters were somewhere in the forest. I wondered if Vincenzo was beyond the barrier waiting for me.

The white wolf, Mathilde, stood and watched us for a few moments, and then it looked as if she winked at me before she ran off.

"Are you ready?" I asked the Countess, before she could say anything I started off towards the house.

The small, dilapidated cottage was so surrounded by enormous trees it was nearly invisible, and would be well hidden even in daylight. I started for the front door and Countess Zrinyi quickly pulled me back and behind a nearby tree.

"You are most definitely a Bathory," she said sharply. "Charging in with no thought of danger. I fear Gabor has been rubbing off on you."

"And what do you suppose we do?" I asked.

"We watch and plan. Find a way in," she replied. "If the front door is the best way we take it. But we must observe before we pounce."

"This is difficult for me, knowing he's so close."

"He is lucky to have someone like you. Love like that is exceptionally rare."

"Did you love Count Zrinyi?" I asked.

"Miklos was involved with my Mother's arrest." She kept her eyes on the cottage. "So was my sister's husband. She has been much more forgiving."

"I am sorry, I did not realise," I replied. "That must have been terrible for your children."

"I have no children."

"How long were you married?"

"Ten years. But my Mother did not have me until she had been...," she began, a quick look at me and she stopped. I knew the story; Erzsebet Bathory did not give Ferenc Nadasdy a child until ten years into their marriage.

What part my Mother's birth played in that situation was a mystery.

I turned my attention back to the house. It looked as if there was only one door.

"I suppose they picked this location on purpose, so they could control as many elements as possible," Countess Zrinyi said as if she had heard my thoughts.

I smiled. "And they kept the beings they believed to have magic as far as they could manage."

"I don't understand," she began, pausing while she considered my statement. "He taught you things, didn't he?"

"Some. Hopefully it's enough to help," I said, standing up fully and coming out of the brush.

I started the largest fires I could on each side of the house, not bothering to try to control them. Someone came out and I used another spell to throw them into the flames.

"If we can get them to let their guard down it would make things easier for us," the Countess said.

"I will try my best," I replied.

I managed to pull the door off its hinges and smash all the windows from a distance while the fires continued. Whoever was in the house seemed undisturbed, so I tried to put my energy into physically moving the building itself.

But I did not have enough power.

"*Now can we go?*" I asked after I made a final attempt to move the structure.

"Do you think you can take two of them alone?" she asked.

"Can you?" I said as she drew her sword and we stalked towards the house.

The woman strode out of the front door of the house like a Queen walking into the great hall of her palace. I could not see her face clearly, the backlight from the fires turning her into a simple figure.

She was dressed in men's clothes with a long cape, her black hair wild and loose as it hung down to her waist. I was reminded of when we first saw Beatrix in Russia and my stomach lurched.

As her eyes turned to me my body grew tense, she came closer and I finally got a look at her face.

"Who are you?" she yelled at me as three others came out behind her.

"I am Katrine Bathory, and you have something that belongs to me," I said angrily. The Countess and I stood our ground. Her presence gave me a new found confidence.

The woman laughed. "I suppose you think your little tricks would scare us?"

"Not really," I replied, shrugging my shoulders. "I mostly needed to get you outside."

I felt the rumble of paws and the low growl as the wolves stepped out of the forest. The woman didn't even flinch.

She drew her sword and stared at the blade as it glimmered in the moonlight.

"Is he worth dying for, Katrine Bathory?" she asked casually.

"I should ask you the same question." My anger flared and I rushed at her, smacking her sword out of the way and reaching for her throat.

She easily knocked me on my back; I used a spell to knock the sword out of her hand and sent it spinning out into the darkness.

I jumped up and dove at her, we wrestled in the grass. She swung at me, her fist connecting with my chin and I felt a crack in my face. I slammed my palm into her nose and blood squirted all over her white skin. She grabbed for my throat, digging the tips of her fingers in deep as she tried to pull the skin out.

I pushed in on her elbow until I heard a snap and she cried out, releasing her grip. I grabbed on to her arm and started to twist it at the shoulder until I felt a pop.

Pretty confident I had broken her arm I picked her up and tried to throw her as far as I could; I thought it would give me enough time to run inside.

But she landed on her feet and came at me again, swinging her arm until the shoulder popped back. She struck me in the shoulder with her forearm and used her good hand to punch me in the jaw again. The crack radiated down my neck and through my face, I hoped she hadn't broken anything.

I felt blood drip down my split lip, the metallic taste in my mouth made me angry.

I was a vampire. A predator.

And above all things, I was a Bathory.

I thought about the vein in her throat and immediately I had her by the neck. She pulled away from me rather easily but I kept coming, caught in the urge to taste her blood. I had lost track of everything else, and when the thirst began to overwhelm me she got the upper hand. She got me on the ground, pinning my body beneath her as she held the knife to my throat with her free hand.

"It has been a while since I killed a vampire." She spat in my face. She was so focused she did not notice I was bending my leg.

"What is your name?" I asked.

"Colombina. Why do you ask?"

"Because if I am to claim responsibility for killing a Cesari I would like to be specific," I said, quickly lifting my leg so I could knee her in the back.

The split second of shock gave me a chance to hit her weak arm, distracting Colombina long enough for me to grab my dagger and shove it into her chin all the way to the hilt.

She stared wide eyed at me as I lifted her off me, the knife still steady in my hand. She began to sputter, blood dripping from the corners of her mouth.

"If you'll pardon me, Colombina, you have taken something

that belongs to me. You better pray he is unharmed," I said in her ear.

Countess Zrinyi had made short work of the others. The wolves were pulling their bodies apart. I heard someone running through the woods and knew that the wall had come down, so I held on to Colombina and waited. I used a spell to put out the fires and I saw Bianca's golden head come out of the darkness.

I pulled Colombina along by the hair and the knife hilt, pulling out the blade and dropping her body at Bianca's feet. I was shocked when Colombina tried to get up. Bianca pushed her back down with her foot.

"Un regalo per voi, sorella più onorato," I said proudly, fighting the compulsion to lick the blood off the blade.

A gift for you, most honoured sister.

"Grazie," she replied. I turned and ran for the house, hoping I was not too late.

A dark heap lay in the corner of the one room house, quiet and motionless. I went to it and only found a pile of rags, then proceeded to tear the house apart.

But he was nowhere to be found.

"William?" I called out. I had sensed him. I kept calling his name and there was only silence. I fell to my knees and screamed.

"Katrine?" Gabriel came running in the door and scooped me into his arms.

"He's not here!" I wailed. "Why is he not here?"

"Please, Katrine, you need to try to calm down and use your senses."

"But I did! And he was here!"

"Please, just try again."

I tried to calm my breathing and as soon as I did I could feel

William as if he was standing right beside me. The thirst began to pull at me.

"I smell blood," Gabriel said flatly.

"I know," I said, and I saw a small drop of something fall onto the floor. I pulled Gabriel over as the red spot began to swell and stain the floorboard.

"My God," Gabriel cursed as I felt him look at the ceiling. I tried to brace myself for what I was about to see; William was strapped to the ceiling as if it was a cross, blood dripping from the lashes on his exposed arms, legs, and chest. I screamed.

"Help me cut him down," I said finally, trying to find chairs for us to stand on.

"Katrine, the blood." Gabriel's voice was strained.

"No!" I yelled. "You are not an animal! You have to control it!"

"Let me call for the others. We will need help getting him down without hurting him," he said as he stumbled outside. I ignored him, pulling a chair into the middle of the room so I could stand on it and cradle his face in my hands.

"I am here, William. Can you hear me? Please, my love. Just open your eyes," I said quietly to him. In an instant his eyes shot open, his gaze of blue fire looking angrily around before turning to me.

"We will cut you down, and we are taking you home. I will never let anyone hurt you again," I said. I stayed with him as the others came in and began making plans to cut him down.

NOT ENOUGH

Colombina lay on the ground, her hands and feet tightly bound. Her chest rose and fell at a steady pace.

"Why is she still breathing?" I was sure my anger was radiating off of me like electricity.

"I will take her back to Naples, so our family can deal with her appropriately," Bianca said.

"That's not good enough!" I turned on her and screamed in her face. "Did you see what she did? She does not leave the forest alive."

"Katrine, there are ways that these situations are supposed to be handled," Bianca was stern as she spoke.

"Fine! Les Vieux are back at the chateau. They can deal with it."

Her eyes lowered. "Les Vieux has no relevance in this situation."

"She is not leaving France alive, Bianca. I found her, I fought her, I handed her to you with the thought you would kill her. And if you will not I will, but that is as far as it goes." I was a short distance from her face as I growled the words at her. "She dies tonight Bianca. Whether you like it or not."

I went to where William lay, Bianca and I had stepped aside

to argue. He lay on several planks of wood that the men had found and would use to carry him back to the carriages.

"Please don't fight," he said softly as I leaned down beside him. "She is only trying to do what my mother would have asked."

"Your mother would let her live?" I asked.

"My mother would want to kill her herself, to send a message."

"Then she should have come herself! I will not allow it," I said sharply, pulling Vincenzo's dagger from the sheath at my ankle.

He grabbed on to my wrist. "If you are the one who kills her, the Cesari will have a vendetta against you."

"I am not worried," I replied, rising and starting towards Colombina.

"Katrine," Countess Zrinyi called my name and I paused. She pulled out her sword and handed it to me, hilt first.

"You clearly haven't killed many people," she said flatly. "Unless you want to be barbaric the sword is much more effective."

The sword was quite heavy and I had to hold it with both hands. I was impressed by how easily she wielded it.

I felt something brush up against my leg as I started to walk. Charles looked up at me through his wolf eyes, I gently pat his head and scratched behind his ears.

"It is his way of showing support," Vincenzo said. I had not noticed him beside me; he and Morgana had been rummaging through the house while the others secured William.

"I would offer to do this for you but I know I cannot," Vincenzo said quietly.

"You came. That is enough," I replied.

"Morgana and I found something in the house," he continued but I had to stop him.

"One thing at a time," I said. He nodded in acknowledgment, following along behind me as I continued.

Colombina had rolled so she could see me. She smiled in a way that reminded me of Klara.

"This is not the end," she said in Italian. "We will not stop until they are all dead."

"You made the mistake of coming after the man I love, and anyone who dares try to hurt him shall pay with their life as you shall pay with yours," I answered her back in her own tongue. She opened her mouth to say more but before she got out a full sentence I swung the sword at her neck. There was a sickening ripping sound and a loud snap as the sword went in, a gurgle and gush of blood as I pulled it through the other side and severed her head from her body.

I stood for a few moments, silently trying to catch my breath as the blood gushed from the open wound.

"Are you alright?" Vincenzo asked.

"Better now. What did you find?" I asked.

"Give Countess Zrinyi back her sword first," he said flatly. I gave her the weapon, and he handed me a torn piece of paper with a fully intact seal attached.

"Look familiar?" he asked.

I shrugged. "No. Should it?"

"Perhaps. It is Beatrix Delphine's seal," he said flatly.

"What do you know of this?" I asked Ivan. "She is one of yours. Is that how you knew where he was?"

"Why do you think she is one of ours?" he asked.

"Don't patronise me, Ivan."

"She may be a member of the Order but she is not one of ours." His expression had turned very serious. "There have been whispers of true evil amongst our ranks, but we have had no proof. A crime such as this will be thoroughly investigated, since it is clearly rooted in secrets. Perhaps you should speak to her sister about such matters. Were you not her protégée?"

"Please let me know the results of your investigation, and thank you again for your help." I shook his hand. "Believe me when I tell you that I will be speaking with Grisela Delphine at the earliest opportunity."

We rode home in silence. Gabriel went with Vincenzo and the others so William could fit in our carriage.

Morgana stared at me from the other side of the carriage, she and Bianca sat on the opposite side.

"Was she involved?" I asked Morgana.

"Who?" she asked, even though I was confident she knew exactly who I was talking about. I rolled my eyes but before I could say anything else she continued.

"I said she could not pull this off on her own, but why would she involve Beatrix?" She looked at William then back at me again.

"Because she's insane! The entire God forsaken family is completely deranged!" My voice grew louder as I got more agitated. William touched my hand to try to calm me down. "If I find out Gigi was involved I will kill her."

"You won't have to. Charles would not tolerate such behaviour, and with Les Vieux already in Paris it would be easy enough to have her executed," William said.

I leaned over and gently kissed his forehead. He smiled weakly at me. I could tell he was in pain.

"I will protect you," I whispered.

He squeezed my hand. "I am the luckiest man alive."

Ivan and Countess Zrinyi were standing across the road, watching as William was loaded into the house. Another carriage arrived shortly after us with Charles, Mathilde, and the other shifters back in human form and fully clothed.

I crossed the street alone and went and stood with them.

"I cannot thank you enough for what you have done. Especially you, Countess Zrinyi. You are truly an admirable woman," I said.

"We are more than happy to help, and perhaps now you can finally see that we are not the enemy," Ivan replied. "We shall investigate the Delphine involvement, please send us word about her sister's reaction. Please do not judge us because of the actions of some misguided individuals."

"I will, you have my word," I said.

"One day we may call on you for assistance." Ivan reminded me.

"And I will come, as long as I have no moral objections."

He smiled. "Which is exactly what I would expect from a Bathory."

I heard Hannah call my name, turning my head for only a moment to wave at her. When I turned back they were gone.

SMILE

I stormed into the chateau, tossing my cloak at Hannah as I moved through the hall into the salon. The crowd parted as if they knew, clearing the way so I had a direct line to Gigi.

She paid me no mind until I was too close for her to react. I grabbed her by the back of her coiffed hairdo and dragged her across the room and into the kitchen.

The maid's quickly cleared out as I pulled Gigi towards the hearth, the fire burning bright.

"What are you doing?!" she shrieked with fear.

"Making a point," I said calmly, pulling her closer to the flame.

"Burning me will make a point about what?"

"They found Beatrix's seal with the witch hunters, Grisela."

"What does that have to do with me?"

I tightened my grip on her hair and pulled her close so our eyes met. "I know you. I know you've been receiving updates on her since we left Russia. You knew this was coming and you let it happen."

She said nothing, only stared at my face in sheer terror.

"You are lucky he's alive," I growled. "Do you have anything to say for yourself?"

"He is lucky to have someone like you," she said flatly.

"Where's Beatrix?" I screamed in her face.

"I don't know," she replied, screaming as I dragged her closer to the flame. "You wouldn't believe me if I told you!"

"Try me."

"I...I knew she was in France meeting with someone, but I did not know they were witch hunters! Do you really think I would be foolish enough to try to kill William of Naples?"

"You were calling me..."

"It has nothing to do with you, you silly ass! I would be quite stupid not to be afraid of *him!* My sister is involved in something..."

"I will find out where Beatrix is, and I will deal with her myself since you are clearly incapable." I dropped her into a pile of ashes at the base of the hearth. "And if I find out you are lying, fire will be the least of your worries."

***

"I am most pleased that you were successful," Prince Radu appeared as I was about to go upstairs.

"Thank you, my Lord," I replied.

"And I apologise for not providing assistance earlier. But I feel that I may be more use to you now," he continued.

I paused. "And how is that?"

"Let me say that the Delphine have quite a reputation, and Les Vieux has been keeping an eye on the entire family for many years. I believe that some current family strife may be the cause of Grisela's mental state."

"So she knows more about Beatrix then she is willing to admit?"

He sighed. "Sadly I believe she does not. She is being quite honest. The Delphine matriarch is aware of everything but does not

152

tell the children details, including her favourite, Grisela. She is quite masterful at putting one child against another, and Beatrix is quite dangerous and hates Grisela. But since the death of the oldest things have been a bit tense.”

“I don't understand.”

“The oldest Delphine child, Esme, one of the three humans, died recently. We were assuming Beatrix was in France en route to England for the funeral.”

I paused, my thoughts beginning to swim. This information explained a lot; the letters in Gigi's room must have been from her mother and the rest of the family.

“I had no idea.” I quietly admitted.

“I suspected as much. It does not appear that Grisela is planning to go to England, but her mother may be requesting such a thing of her favourite because she cannot go, being in her ninetieth year and looking no older than her twenty fifth.”

“Why would Gigi not tell me? She said that she knew her sister was involved with something, and the other members of The Order mentioned evil in their midst.”

“There is talk, Katrine. Talk of a group from the Order that have turned to the side of evil. They wish to bring forth Hell on to this earth, and they are trying to find ways to do so. I fear that Grisela somehow plays a part in their plans. I do not have much information, but when I do I will inform you. But, the point I am trying to get at is that we can help you find Beatrix, if you wish.”

“What would I have to do for you in return?”

He laughed. “I am a man of honour, Mademoiselle Bathory. You saved my daughter's life and her guardian's as well. I am more than happy to come to your aid. All I will suggest is that Beatrix Delphine is a criminal, and you have witnessed how we deal with criminals.”

“And what will become of me should I choose to.....dispose of a threat on my own, my Lord?”

“That is entirely your choice, my dear. But beware of this evil.

You would need to protect yourself from the family. Les Vieux would be grateful for the assistance."

"I apologise, my Lord, but I must go and tend to William. Can we speak about this further, perhaps tomorrow?" I asked.

"Yes, yes, of course. I hope he has a speedy recovery," he said, I bowed to him and quickly went upstairs.

"Katrine," William's voice was strong as I entered the room, Hannah and another servant finished getting him comfortable as Bianca supervised.

"I am here," I said, pulling a small chair over so I was right at his bedside.

"Is Gigi dead?"

"Not yet. Why?"

"That is not necessary at this moment. If either she or Beatrix were involved I had no sign of it."

I hesitated, then said, "The situation will be investigated, my love. It has to, even if only to discover how they got in and a way to remedy the security issue."

He took my hand in his. They were cold against my gloves.

"Bianca said you killed a Cesari," he said.

"She tried to take you from me. She does not get to live," I replied, biting back tears. I had to cover my mouth and try to calm my breathing. I did not want to show the others how terrified I was.

"Leave us," William said sharply, clearing the room so we were alone. The tears broke through then and I started to sob. I lay my head on the bed beside him and he stroked my hair.

"I shall have to thank Gabriel for his assistance," he said. "Bianca told me about the others. Do not hold Vincenzo's initial reaction against him, the Cesari have earned their reputation. If you had not come when you did..."

"Don't say it!" I grabbed on to his hand. "You are here and

you are safe. That is what matters."

"I am sorry that you had to deal with this, il mio amore. But it is an unfortunate curse of my family. I am sorry I did not tell you, but it is a hard thing to explain."

"I have killed one of them. I am part of this now. I am sure they will come after me too."

He smiled. "We shall have to face this together, then."

"The idea that I could have lost you, and no one would help me other than Gabriel...I was so lost and alone. I would not survive without you, William," I kissed his hand, "and I will not let you out of my sight. I do not care about what is proper."

He chuckled. "None of that would matter if we got married."

"Right. Then we shall get married tomorrow."

"Oh no no, I will not have you do this on impulse because you are frightened."

"It is not an impulse. It is a realisation of the truth. I want to be married to you. I want to share your bed. I want to wake up beside you. I want to just be with you. Is that so wrong?" I started, and more tears followed. He wiped the tears from my cheeks with his fingers; he tried to move to kiss my face and groaned in pain. I stood up and kissed him, he cupped my face with his hands.

"I do not want to be anything if it's not with you," I whispered to him, he shed a few tears himself.

I arranged the bed so he could lie comfortably, and then crawled in beside him, lying on top of the covers and curling myself around his body. We lay together in silence, holding each other so closely I thought our heart beats had fallen into synch. I listened closely to the sounds of his body, and the rhythmic rise and fall of his chest as he took breath.

When I knew he was asleep I began to relax, the weight of the day's events started to fall away like specks of dirt. My own exhaustion started to take over, the warmth and comfort of William's presence easing me to sleep.

A TIME AND PLACE

I felt William quickly inhale, then his hot breath on my face as he pulled me closer to him, until my ear was pressed against his chest and I could feel his steady heartbeat in my head.

I hoped that when he awoke and found me sleeping next to him he realised how serious I was. Proper decorum and marriage be damned, the time he had been gone had terrorised me enough that I would not let him out of my sight.

And I would find Beatrix and tear her throat out with my teeth.

I heard the bedroom door open and close quietly and I knew immediately it was Hannah, with Vincenzo and Bianca close behind.

William adjusted himself so he was sitting upright while I continued to feign sleep.

"Is she alright, my Lord?" Hannah asked William quietly. I wondered if she would be distraught by my actions, being so concerned with protecting my virtue.

But it was clear that we had both slept fully clothed, William under covers and I on top. I would reassure her that my virtue will remain intact until my wedding night when we were alone.

"I believe so. Exhausted, but well," he said. "Thank you for the food, Hannah. I will send for you when Katrine wakes."

"Of course." She nodded and quickly left the room.

"She dragged Grisela by her hair into the kitchen hearth," Vincenzo said in Italian. "She's not burnt, but the way she complains about soot on a dress you'd think Katrine had set her on fire."

"She's lucky she's not dead." Bianca sounded amused. "Your paramour has quite the temper, brother."

"Her temper saved my life and killed one of the strongest living Cesari." William was sharp, as if his sister's thoughts on me irritated him.

"Tis not a complaint. I admire her greatly. You have chosen better than I had expected, considering the past..."

William cut his sister off. "That is not important. What did you find out?"

"Beatrix's seal was at the scene. The Cesari were all dead before we could question them," Vincenzo replied. "But I will ask some of our contacts. You will have to ask Katrine, but I believe Prince Radu has offered his assistance."

William adjusted himself in bed. "She will go after Beatrix regardless of what anyone else says, so we must help where we can. And Vincenzo, I must speak with our jeweller as soon as I am able."

I could hear Vincenzo smile when he said, "She has finally agreed to marry you, il mio amico?"

"You would not dare wed without our parents present, William!" Bianca exclaimed.

"Then you better send for them, for I fear she will not want to wait long," William told her.

I thought about opening my eyes and telling him that he and I would wait in this bed while preparations were made, if need be.

"You may have time. She will most likely want to be sure there are no other threats before going ahead. And you will have to speak to Gabriel," Vincenzo said, chuckling to himself. "Be thankful you no longer need Grisela's permission...but in that case you may need mine!"

"Do you think she could kill this Beatrix?" Bianca asked. "Because now that she is to be a Santorini perhaps we should approach this as a family. She killed several Cesari, with the aid of that woman."

"What woman?" William and Vincenzo asked in unison.

"Did you both think a member of the Order of the Dragon would stand by and do nothing?" Bianca seemed confused. "What is her name! She said she was Gabriel's cousin..."

"Countess Zrinyi helped Katrine kill the Cesari?" William asked.

"Yes! She jumped through the barrier to go after her and everything. I would have gone myself, and I did try," she explained. "Katrine used Countess Zrinyi's blade to kill Colombina."

I knew without even looking that William and Vincenzo were exchanging confused glances. I still did not quite believe it. In my heart I knew to take it for what it was. She had helped complete a task. Thinking about it too deeply would only cause heartache.

I started to stir, hoping it would stop the men from explaining their shock to Bianca. This was not a conversation I wanted to have yet.

I opened my eyes and stared up at William, who smiled happily at me.

"Good, you are awake," he said. "Did you sleep well?"

"Never better," I replied, sitting up slightly so I could see Vincenzo. "Good morning."

"Good morning, mon ami. I am glad to see that you are well," Vincenzo said.

"I will be better when we are married and Beatrix is dead," I answered flatly. "Did you know that Esme Delphine is dead?"

He stopped, thinking for a moment. "No, but you'll have to remind me which one that is. I fear there are more Delphine's than the world can take."

"Apparently she's the oldest and one of the humans."

He thought again, and then said, "I have heard of her, but was unaware that she had passed. It would certainly explain Gigi's state."

"I care very little about her state, but it may be why Beatrix is in France. If she is on her way to the funeral she would have to pass through to get to England," I began. "So we will have to move quickly if that is the case. I won't chase her around the continent."

"Of course. When the two of you have risen for the day we shall discuss going to meet with some contacts," Vincenzo said.

"And I shall write to the family in the meantime. Mother is probably feverish with worry," Bianca added, quickly leaving the room. I had not thought of where she would end up now that William was in his own bed.

"Prince Radu believes he can find her," I said to Vincenzo once the bedroom door had closed.

"What were you trying to achieve by dragging Gigi into the kitchen hearth?" He was clearly angry with me.

"I wasn't going to kill her," I replied. He had never spoken to me in such a way. I was a bit shocked.

"Am I being scolded?" I asked.

"I understand you are angry, Katrine, but I will *not* condone reckless behaviour, do you understand? No girl of mine will go on a murderous rampage without proper planning!" Vincenzo yelled.

I smiled at him. "I apologise, mon ami. I shall try to keep my rage to a dull roar."

He slowly let out his breath. "Hopefully it scared some sense into her. Now, you two eat and make ready. There is much to be done."

He left the room without another word, and I lay back down as soon as we were alone. William pulled me into his arms so my head was back against his chest.

"I am ashamed to admit that I did not believe you would stay.

I was shocked to wake beside you," William said quietly.

"You'll grow accustom to it, over time. I am sure," I replied.

"And now I am not sure I want to leave."

"Are you well?"

"That is not why I wish to stay."

"I know, but I am concerned that you are not well enough to go."

"A few cuts and bruises cannot keep me down, il mio amore. We shall do this together."

I moved my head so I could look him in the eyes. "You may help with the fight but Beatrix Delphine dies by my hand. Do you understand?"

He paused, and then gently kissed my forehead. "As you wish."

The four of us rode in silence; Bianca had stayed behind to write home and Morgana had decided to come along.

"I feel fine," William said. His eyes lowered in Morgana's direction.

"I am not willing to take the chance that you are not. With your sister staying behind it's a necessity," Morgana replied sharply.

"We're only going to see a contact. I am sure it will not be dangerous," Vincenzo added.

"Now is not the time to take chances, mon ami," I said flatly. Then we returned to silence.

The carriage rattled through the streets of Paris. Vincenzo said we were going to talk to a witch, and I wondered if it was the one we'd met at the market.

We got out next to small wood house just steps from the river, and I got the impression that things were distinctively different.

A woman opened the front door and scowled at us, she looked about 35 years old.

"I did not realise you were bringing an entire caravan," the woman said, ushering us inside.

"I apologise, Madam, we would not all be here if it was not urgent," I said to her as she brought us into the main room.

Her eyes turned to William. "I am pleased to see you are well, Monsieur."

"And I suppose you are the woman who went after him? He is lucky to have someone like you, Mademoiselle," she smiled brightly at me. "Now, why have you come? I thought the witch hunters were dead."

"They are. I am looking for the person who brought them here," I said. "A woman named Beatrix Delphine."

She spat on the floor and called Beatrix the devil, her expression filled with anger and hatred.

"What is your name, if I may ask?" I asked her.

"Lydia."

"Lydia, my name is Katrine. It sounds as if you and I have an enemy in common. Have you ever been in love?"

She gulped in a big breath. "Yes I have."

"So then I am sure you can understand my need to harm those who have tried to hurt those I love? The first time she did something it was a bit indirect, but this has changed everything. She *will* pay for what she has done."

Her brow furrowed, and then she said, "I *insist* on preparing something for you."

She took out a brass plate similar to the one Vincenzo bought in the market and began mixing herbs and some liquid in the centre.

"Do you know how to find her?" I asked as we all stood in silence and watched her.

"She is not alone. She has strong spell casters who travel with her. And Luka," Lydia said. I watched her as she continued on. Something had changed after she said his name.

"Did you love Luka Tornovitch, Lydia?" I asked. She did

not reply, the force she used to crush the herbs was enough. She finished mixing and poured the liquid into a small vial, once she had secured the stopper she handed it to me.

"The last I heard was that they are staying at a chateau close to the main city gates," Lydia said.

"Merci," I replied.

I turned to leave and she grabbed my wrist. "If I hear anything else I shall send word. Thank you for being strong where others could not."

I squeezed her hand, then turned and walked out.

"We came for the potion, didn't we?" I said to Vincenzo. "You knew exactly what she would say, didn't you?"

He smiled. "Lydia is a good woman. What they did to her was terrible."

"She did not exactly give us a location, mon ami. I am unsure which gates are considered the 'main gates' to the city as well," I replied.

"I am more concerned with the strong spell casters. I am sure either Radu or the Order knows *exactly* where she is," he said. "And I pray you are not naive enough to think the Order will allow you to kill one of their own."

I smiled. "It does not matter what I think; only what they *believe* I think. I have a plan."

"I sincerely hope so," he replied as we climbed back into the carriage.

GATHERING

Charles rose as we entered the library. Mathilde and Victorie were seated beside him.

"What's going on?" I asked.

"We protect our own," Victorie said sharply while staring up at Charles.

"I cannot allow you to go after Beatrix alone!" Charles proclaimed.

"I am not alone!" I snapped at him.

He rolled his eyes. "I know I made a mistake not acting quickly and I sincerely apologise for that, but the reality is that this is *my organization*. Actions such as that are not made without my knowledge and involvement. You will not charge off alone."

"What about Grisela?" I asked.

"Believe it or not, she understands the seriousness of the situation. And she is well aware of the fact that I will not tolerate an attack on our people, and if it was discovered that she had a hand in this." His eyes turned away for a moment. I could hear the anger rising in his voice. "Besides, I would lock her in the underground without a second thought if she tried to complain. It would not be the first time."

"And if I may say, Mademoiselle," Prince Radu's voice came out of the darkness, "if our information is correct you will need all the help you can get."

He and Sybilla came into the light; they had been standing in one of the far corners of the room. I was shocked to see how similar they actually looked.

"Where is she?" I asked Radu, finally meeting his eyes.

"I believe your friends at the Order are trying to intervene," he replied.

"They are the reason William is alive," I said angrily. "Keep that in mind before you continue."

"If they know you are coming she will be warned. We don't know who is with her and who is not within the Order."

I sighed in frustration. "If she is foolish enough to believe she can attack William and I would not come after her she is less intelligent than I thought. She knows I am coming, my Lord. I can guarantee it. What they tell her is irrelevant."

"So you know she will be expecting you and you are fine with that?"

"She cannot be moved, my Lord," Vincenzo said. "All we can do is support her decision."

"And we will. We protect our own," Victorie added, loud enough so the whole room took notice.

"Thank you," I said to her, smiling and nodding at Mathilde as well. I had seen her in the forest. I was truly grateful.

"What is your plan, Katrine?" Charles asked. He watched me intently, his brown eyes full of determination and focus.

I turned back to Radu. "Where is she?"

"I will send word to the others that you are ready to move. When they arrive we can go," he replied.

"We must wait until Gabriel rises. I will not go without him," I said flatly. "At sundown we shall make our move."

***

Vincenzo sat beside me as I sat on one of the couches in the library, fingering the vial Lydia had given me.

"Remind me never to anger you," he told me quietly.

"I would go to such great lengths for you as well. I hope you know that," I said. He took my free hand and squeezed it.

"Is it worth it if she kills you?"

I smiled. "Perhaps she will learn not to threaten Gigi or anyone associated with her again."

"You would still defend her after all she has done?"

"The two of you saved my life. That is not something that simply goes away." I looked away from him. I felt her presence in the room, she did not come closer. I suppose she was trying to keep a safe distance.

"You know I cannot come with you, ma petite," Gigi's voice was soothing and melodic. "It is a very complicated time in our family."

"I am sorry for your loss," I said. I did not turn and look at her, but spoke out into the room.

"We all know that humans die, but it is still tragic when it happens," she said softly. "Beatrix had no love for my sister but that does not mean she will not use it. Do not forget that she is ruthless, and always know you will have to upstage her in everything to achieve your goal."

"I intend to kill her for what she has done."

"And I pray you are successful," she said, and then quietly left the room.

"I apologise for that," Vincenzo said once she was gone.

"No need, mon ami. I knew it would come eventually," I replied.

There was a light knock at the door then Tolone came in, he tried to smile but his fear was not easy to hide.

"Les Vieux has arrived, and they are requesting your presence, Mademoiselle," Tolone said.

"Thank you, Tolone. Please tell Hannah I would like to speak with her," I replied.

He smiled. "She is just outside the room waiting to speak with you."

Vincenzo and Tolone took their leave, sending Hannah in. I went to her and hugged her tightly.

"Are you alright, Katrine?" Hannah's voice was full of confusion.

"Yes I am. And I wanted to reassure you that my virtue is fully intact and will remain so until my wedding day," I said as I pulled away from her. "Which will be happening soon, by the way. So when this is over you and I will being preparations."

She smiled widely. "Are you certain?"

"Bianca is writing home to tell the family to come to Paris. So when they arrive..."

"Oh, how wonderful!" she exclaimed, clapping her hands in delight. "Something magical has come from all this madness!"

"Yes, and after tonight this particular madness will be over, and I pray things calm down for a while. There has been far too much drama for my liking since Roza died," I replied. "Now, if you'll excuse me, my company has arrived."

All eyes turned to me as I entered the salon, as an army would upon sight of their general.

I first noticed Suren, dressed in a heavy black uniform with her hair in two long plaits, the dark shiny colour in stark contrast to the dull texture of the uniforms fabric. She looked like a true warrior.

"It is traditional Mongol dress for a soldier," she said to me.

"It is very distinguished. I wish I had something similar," I told her.

She smiled. "I believe one day you will."

Prince Radu stepped forward. "We have located her, Mademoiselle."

"Thank you, my Lord. Has my cousin rose for the day?" I asked.

"I am here." Gabriel's voice rang out as he stepped forward from the back of the room. "What is your plan?"

"She walked right in our front door in Russia. I suppose we shall do the same." I began, raising my voice and proclaiming to the room. "Now, anyone who does not wish to come may stay behind and guard the chateau. It will not be held against you."

I put out my hand. William stepped forward and took it in his, twining our fingers together. Without another word we headed out, the others following along behind.

IN FORMATION

The simple stone house stood close to what I recognised as the main gates to Paris, I suppose for a simple entrance and exit for its occupants. With no obvious signs of life, the darkness of the building blended seamlessly with the night sky.

"Perhaps they turned tail and ran," Mathilde said. I closed my eyes and pushed out my senses, building a vision of the house in my mind as I scanned it and the surrounding area.

"She's here, with two spell casters and several others....four guards. All vampires," I replied.

"We shall take the outside," Mathilde said. Gabriel took her hand and softly kissed her knuckles, whispering something to her as she and the other shifters walked off into a small wooded area.

"Do not worry. We can handle it." Charles kissed my hand then following the other shifters.

"Morgana," I said, and she came up to stand beside me. "Can you knock the door clean off its hinges?"

"Gladly," she replied. She lifted up her hand, wiggling her fingers as her lips moved; the door exploded, splintered wood flew wildly in the air.

I went forward, quickly moving up the stairs and stepping

through the hole where the door had been.

"Come out, come out, wherever you are," I mumbled to myself as I strode through the dark hallway. All I found was silence.

I kicked open the basement door, before I could continue on Finn Hawk pushed ahead and disappeared down into the darkness. Others followed behind him, so I decided to go upstairs.

I felt Beatrix's presence as I moved. She stood in the room at the back of the house in the dark, staring out the window.

I crept up slowly behind her, trying to be sure there was no one else in my path. I had not thought beyond finding her.

"I was hoping you would come," she said flatly without turning around.

"I am shocked you would think I wouldn't, considering what you did to William," I replied. I stepped through the doorway and scanned the room. We were alone.

"I had to get your attention."

"There are better ways."

"Not to prove my point."

"And that would be?"

"You do not belong with them, you belong with the Order. And your faith is misplaced in my sister."

I laughed. "You really have no idea, do you?"

"What do you mean?"

"The Order helped me find William. And if you are one of them, why did they not come to stop me from killing you? Perhaps it is your faith that is misguided. Perhaps whatever evil you are involved with is not as good as you imagined."

"Where is my sister?"

"She has cast me aside."

Beatrix laughed. "You are not the first. Now you may understand why I feel so inclined to take her from this earth. But she plays a greater part in what is to come. You'll see."

"You will not get that far. You have attacked those I love.

For what you did to William you deserve a painful death."

She paused. "He is lucky to have someone like you. So was Grisela. She shall learn the error in her ways I am sure of it."

"I appreciate the sentiment," I said, preparing myself for an attack.

"You said I deserve to die for what I have done, Katrine. I am surprised you still think so naively." She turned around to face me. "You need to face what you are, and understand we do not live as humans do, we live *from* them. It is because of their blood that we are able to survive. You are a monster, just like me. We are all part of the darkness and the sooner you come to terms with that the easier it will be. And I shall bring darkness down on this earth like no one has ever seen, unleashing true Hell on earth!"

"I am nothing like you!" I screamed at her. I lunged, knocking her to the ground.

She easily threw me off and I crashed into a wall. I had enough time to stand before she came at me again. I was able to fling her off but not far enough. She quickly rebalanced herself and stood.

"Do you really think you can beat me? That you could kill me so easily?" she shouted in my face. She knocked me to the ground and we wrestled as she got her hands around my throat.

I began to feel light headed as she tightened her grip, choking the air out of me. Then, suddenly, my mind became very clear and all I could see was William's face, and hear his voice telling Bianca to write home and tell his parents to come to Paris for our wedding.

I flipped us over so Beatrix was flat on her back. I punched her as hard as I could in the jaw which caused her to release her grip.

I smacked her nose with my palm which let out a spray of blood, giving me enough time to grab Lydia's potion out of my sleeve and dump the contents of the vial in Beatrix's mouth.

"A gift from someone who you stole something precious from," I growled in her face. "She sends her regards."

She threw me off, laughing to herself.

"I see you have met Lydia," Beatrix said as she pulled herself to her feet. "I hope you were not relying on that potion. They are not always effective."

I grabbed Vincenzo's knife from my ankle sheath and plunged it into her chest.

"I am not as naive as you think, Beatrix," I said as she collapsed to the floor. I pulled the knife out and blood began to squirt from her chest.

"Katrine!" William's voice called as he came bounding into the room. I put my blade away. He stopped as he stared down at Beatrix's body while she began to choke.

"So that is her?" he asked.

"Was," I said flatly.

"The house is clear. It's time to go," he replied. I turned my head and cast one of the spells he had taught me, and small fires began to catch throughout the room.

I held out my hand to him, and he continued to set small fires as we walked out of the house together.

He rubbed his thumb along mine as we stood together, hand in hand, and watched the house burn.

"Is she dead?" Prince Radu asked from his place to my left. "Did you watch her die?"

"I stabbed her, and then we set the house ablaze as she lay bleeding on the floor. I cannot imagine she survived," I replied. "I also fed her a potion from a witch."

"But you did not see the moment of her death?"

"No. Why?" I turned my eyes away from the house to look at him.

"If there had been no fire I would have been concerned. A knife wound does not guarantee death in our world." He kept his eyes on the house. "But the fire..."

A fireball erupted from the house as the structure began to collapse. I did not ask about what else had been inside.

I had done what I had set out to do.

"That is quite a fire," Morgana's voice came from somewhere behind me. I did not turn to face her but continued to watch the blaze.

"Is everything alright?" I asked her.

"Yes. But it all seemed too simple. As if she planned for this result."

"She had planned to burn?"

"I fear it's much more complicated," she said quietly. "I have visions, but they are unclear."

The house continued to crumble under the heat of the fire; we soon decided to leave, concerned that eyes could be watching us.

The next morning Vincenzo, William and I took a carriage and rode out to see Lydia.

She appeared overjoyed when she saw us, squealing with glee when she opened her front door and found us on her doorstep. She pulled me into her arms and hugged me tightly.

"You are like a beautiful angel!" she said into my hair. "I have never been so happy to see another person."

I laughed. "But I have not even told you if I succeeded?"

"You would not be here if you had not, in some part. Now, come in, please!" she replied, ushering us all inside.

"What exactly does that potion you gave me do?" I asked as we all gathered in the house's main room.

Lydia smiled. "It will turn her into a rotting corpse, working its way from the inside. So if, God forbid, whatever happened did not work the potion will do the job. And she will not see it coming," she laughed again. "She probably said my potions don't work, didn't she? Well, she is in for quite the surprise!"

"Mama?" a small boy's voice said from the open back doorway.

Lydia motioned him forward, and a small Luka Tornovitch stepped into the room.

"Le petit Luc, these are Mama's friends. Mademoiselle Katrine, Signor Amori and Signor di Napoli. Say hello Luc," Lydia said proudly. "These people sent the bad woman who took Papa to Hell."

"Are you angels?" Luc asked me.

I kneeled down so the boy and I were at eye level and said, "No, Luc. We just believe in having good things in this world."

He ran into my arms, wrapping his little hands around my neck. He smelt of dirt and apples, I felt a hot tear roll down my cheek as I hugged him.

He stepped away and smiled, he was missing two of his top teeth.

"I think you are an angel, maybe God has not told you yet," he proclaimed, and then he turned and ran back outside.

"You have done a wonderful thing. Not just for me, but for my son," Lydia said.

"If God had any involvement then we were successful," I replied. "We will take our leave, for now, but I am sure we shall meet again."

She took my hand in hers and gripped it tightly. "If you should need anything at all, do not hesitate. Do you understand?"

"Of course," I said, and she and I bowed to each other before the men and I left.

"Did you know?" I asked Vincenzo once the carriage got moving.

"Know what?" he asked.

"About the boy."

"No, I did not. Would it have made any difference?"

I paused, considering. "No, but it does make it all much sweeter."

"Now that all the messy business is done, we can start planning our wedding," William said. I took his hand. I could not stop myself from smiling.

"Yes, my love. On to better things."

UNEXPECTED

The next morning I received a note from Countess Zrinyi, asking me to meet her alone at the Notre Dame Cathedral at sunset.

"Do you think that is wise?" William asked after he read the note. I'd handed it to him as we lay in his bed. It came in with our morning meal.

"I thought Notre Dame was a safe place, Gigi told me that when I first arrived in Paris," I replied.

"Perhaps that is a myth."

"Perhaps she just wants to speak with me, and that is the most private place she could think of."

"Shall you invite her to the wedding?"

"I suppose. She is family and all. Gabriel would want her there."

"What do you think she wants?"

"I do not know. But there is only one way to find out."

I had not been out alone in such a fashion, and when I sped out into the night it was nice to be with my thoughts. I was concerned, if she told me I had not succeeded in killing Beatrix I did not know how I would react. Or perhaps she was giving me a formal declaration of war, the Order having decided to wipe the Danse Macabre from the planet.

Les Vieux had sanctioned the killing. The Order could answer to them if it came to that.

The carriage pulled up in a line out front of the cathedral. I wrapped a shawl around my hair and made my way to the large wooden doors.

It has been quite a while since I had set foot in a church. Never in my life had I seen a house of worship so grand. Massive multi coloured glass windows, ceilings that I felt quite confidently touched the gates of Heaven themselves they were so high. Whoever built this awe inspiring place would surely be one of His chosen.

I walked slowly up the centre aisle, scanning the room for signs of Countess Zrinyi. I finally sat about midway from the front, where I could examine the altar without seeming peculiar.

"You remind me so much of Kata," Countess Zrinyi said. "She loved all the church decorations and was enchanted by fine embroidery. I miss her so."

She had startled me a little bit. She had sat down so quietly beside me I had not noticed. I wondered if sneaking up on people was something the Order practiced.

"I am flattered by such a comparison," I replied, confident in my belief that when she said Kata she meant her younger sister.

"I wonder how she is fairing, with Gabor and I gone." Her voice was heavy with sadness.

"Grandmother said Kata's husband was trying to steal her inheritance," I said quietly, wondering if it was foolish to mention our connection.

She exhaled loudly. "Do not fret, it is alright that you know, better it be the truth then some ridiculous lie. But her husband did not succeed, and my brother is a fiercely loyal young man and will take care of Kata, should the need arise. Gyorgy does genuinely care for her, so she is better off than most."

"Which reminds me, I would be honoured if you would attend my upcoming nuptials," I said proudly.

"The sorcerer almost dying has scared you good!"

"No. I have always intended to marry him. The experience with the Cesari only showed me that my reasons for delay are foolish."

"Well, I would be happy to attend but I am not sure I will be in Paris. That is why I asked you to come meet me, Katrine. We believe we may have found your Mother."

My breath caught in my throat and I barely managed to say, "Oh."

"There have been some attacks in Upper Hungary, close to one of the Bathory estates. The reports state that some of the peasants have seen a woman who changes into a beast. Of course they believe it to be The Beast of Csejthe. She looks so much like my Mother they fear it is her curse and that she is trying to destroy their crops. I specifically asked to go." She eyes remained forward. "I am hoping that while I am there because of my new.... circumstances I can discover the truth about her conception."

"What shall you, I mean you in the collective sense, do when you find her?" I asked, my voice was quiet and small. I had asked while in Russia that the Order go and help my Mother. I wondered if that was why they were going.

"I do not know. It depends, I suppose, on if she attacks us," she replied. "But I do not want you to get your hopes up that your Mother will be returned to you as she once was."

"I know that is quite impossible, but I appreciate your concern. Thank you, Countess, for being so considerate of me. I only wish to know what has happened to her."

"I will do my best."

"Countess?" I said as she rose to leave. She sat back down,

her eyes focused on the altar.

"Did we succeed? In dealing with Beatrix Delphine, I mean? I do not wish to involve you in this mess, but there was some dispute as to whether or not I was successful."

"I know very little of the details, but I cannot confidently say she is no longer a concern. We have made some progress in finding those she has allied with among us, but we are far from clearing up the problem." She took my hand and squeezed it in hers. "But do not let her ruin your happiness. Marriage for love is a beautiful thing."

We sat for a few minutes staring at the altar, our hands clutched together. She released me first, and before I could say more she was gone. For a moment I worried she would not be able to find my wedding if she was able to attend, then thought better of it.

Countess Zrinyi was a member of the Order of the Dragon. Finding things seemed to be their speciality.

I was happy for more silence on the ride home. The idea that my Mother had got back to Hungary was quite shocking, perhaps that was where the cave from my vision was located. Roza had said Grandmother had given birth to her in the mountains of Hungary, perhaps my Mother somehow knew, and she'd gone there looking for answers.

I imagined that Grandmother was smiling down from Heaven, pleased with the idea that Anna Zrinyi was going to look for my Mother. The thought that Gabriel should go along crossed my mind, but I did not think he would ever go for it. He would not leave me for anything, especially now.

Sybilla was waiting for me in my room when I returned and went to ready for the evening. She was sitting on my bed, wringing her hands together and so lost in thought she did not hear me until

I closed the bedroom door.

"Something wrong, mon ami?" I asked, sitting in the chair by the window.

"Oh, so many things! I am not sure of where to begin," she exclaimed, her eyes glossy with unshed tears.

"My father wishes me to go with him."

"But that is wonderful news!"

"It is a lovely thought but I have no desire to go. And, in part, if not entirely, because I am in love," she said, and she burst into tears.

"Love is a beautiful thing, Sybilla."

"Yes, when you love a man who knows you exist and loves you back!" she blubbered, and my chest began to hurt. I did not want to kill my friend if she was in love with William, but I would if she became a threat.

"And who is this lucky man?"

"Oh, you will think I'm a fool!"

"Sybilla, please."

"It's...it's...oh, it does not matter because he is in love with that bloody little Russian girl, with her perfect blonde hair and stupid...."

"You're in love with Lord Westwick?"

She smiled, the tears still falling. "And if I leave now, he will never...it is so foolish, isn't it? He has not even noticed me. But Katrine, oh dear, I just can't stand it!"

I pulled my friend into my arms and hugged her as she sobbed. I could not figure out for the life of me how, out of all people, Sybilla could fall in love with Charles.

"Would you like me to speak with him on your behalf?" I asked as I pat her head gently.

She stopped and said, "Would you?" then reconsidered, quickly adding, "That would be a terrible act of desperation, don't you think?"

"Natalia did not seem to think so when she asked, not because she loves him but because she did not want to have relations with him and it seemed to work out just fine." I told her. "So your path is clear in regards to her. Perhaps you should make yourself available to him so he can really *see* you, but I must warn you he has a reputation as a womaniser..."

I paused when I felt her body shake, trying to figure out what she was doing.

"Sybilla, are you laughing?" I asked. She sat up, a glowing smile on her wet face.

"I knew I could count on your not to judge me," she said happily. "Perhaps I will try your suggestions."

"How could he not be enchanted by you, mon ami? You are an exceptional woman with lots to offer."

She smiled wider. "I am, aren't I?"

We both stood and helped her straighten herself out.

"I am going to ask Hannah to help me ready for the salon tonight. Do you mind?" she asked as she readied to leave.

"Not at all! I would be honoured and I am sure she would be as well, anything to help you feel your best," I said. We embraced as we stepped out into the hallway, she quickly hurried off but something caught my eye as I headed towards William's room.

Gigi's door was open a crack, a beam of white light was shining out into the hallway. As I stepped closer I saw that her entire room had been redecorated in white, and she was in front of her toilette in a white mourning dress.

"Katrine!" she said, turning to smile at me as I stepped further into the doorway. "I am so pleased to see you."

"You are wearing a mourning dress." The statement came out quite flatly.

"Yes, it seems I have much to mourn. Not only my dear sister Esme, but la reine Margot as well."

"The Queen is dead?"

She laughed. "No, my dear. Do you remember the woman I took you to see, the last Valois? She has passed on."

I was shocked. "*Longue vie à la reine.* I am surprised there was no ceremony for one such as Marguerite de Valois. When did she die?"

"Not long after we saw her," Gigi said, turning away from me. I thought to ask her how long she had known, why she did not tell me, but decided against it. I had no right to do that anymore.

"I am sorry for your loss," I said.

"Thank you," she replied softly. I backed out of the room and left her to her thoughts.

I continued on down the hallway to William's room. I had truly had enough of this day.

THE ARRIVAL

In a manner of weeks William's immediate family were in Paris and the wedding preparations were in full swing.

Every day I walked past Gigi's door; I desperately wanted her advice on so many things, but it was obvious her mind was slowly slipping away from her. My heart broke every time she stepped into the salon in full mourning dress.

Hannah was in her element, and before I knew it I had a wedding gown of sky blue Venetian silk embroidered with symbols of blessings along the skirts hem. Every stitch she had done by hand.

A small church outside the city walls was where the ceremony would take place, my devout Catholic soon to be in-laws insisted on it.

And dear, sweet Gabriel took on the role of my father and mother with such fervor I was in awe. He did not want me to feel as if I was missing out because it was only he and I. I did not mention it to him, since his actions made me feel truly blessed, but I held on to the hope that Countess Zrinyi would end up coming after all.

The day came quickly, and when I woke that morning in my own bed, the first time since his rescue I had slept without William, I was immediately uncomfortable.

When I rose and went to leave my room Hannah was blocking the doorway.

"And where do you think you're going?" Hannah snapped. "You cannot see your groom until you walk down the aisle!"

"I need to know he is alright," I said.

"He is fine, Katrine."

I sat down on my bed and began to fiddle with my ring. "I apologise. This is the first time since he was taken I have not been able to see with my own eyes."

She ran her hands through my hair, brushing it from my face.

"I understand, child. But you will just have to trust me," she said softly. She lay out a tray of food in front of me then began organising my things.

"Shall no one else come to be with me while I ready?" I asked.

"Traditionally your family would, and since it is improper for your cousin to come you are stuck with me."

I smiled. "And, in truth, I would want nothing more. But, I'm curious, where are Morgana and Sybilla?"

"Prince Radu came to collect Sybilla this morning. She mentioned something about a gown for the wedding. I have only seen Morgana briefly as she crossed the kitchen and went into the basement." Hannah did not look at me as she spoke, she was too busy moving around the room organizing my things. "She seemed very determined, her expression was quite dark. You will be pleased to hear that Mademoiselle Delphine rose this morning in good spirits and she is putting forth a real effort to dress for the wedding."

"And what of you, my devoted companion? I hope you have something prepared for yourself?"

She smiled. "Signor Amori insisted. He got something for Father and I, far too grand in my opinion but you have no need to worry. No detail has been ignored."

"Splendid," I replied, nodding slowly. "Will you eat with me?"

"Sure, but before I can I must check on your bath. I won't be a moment," she said, going quickly out into the hall and returning rather quickly.

I wore my hair loose, with pearls woven through the front in such a manner it appeared as if they had grown from the dark strands. The effect was stunning, almost angelic, and suited my blue dress perfectly. Everything was falling into place.

"I never would have dreamed I could look this way," I said when I finally stood and admired my reflection in its entirety. "It's perfect, Hannah. I don't know how to thank you."

"Being present when you get to marry the man you love is enough for me, Katrine," she said proudly. "Now, I must go and ready myself! I will be back soon, and I am sure your cousin will be here as soon as he can."

She kissed my cheek and left, I had to fight the urge to go and see William. I was left alone with my thoughts. It was a good time to contemplate the end of my unattached life.

Was it a fair trade, being able to marry for love but have none of my family present? William would now be my family, and together we will build a new life.

I was lucky in so many *other* ways. And I had Gabriel.

Now, it seemed, no matter what happened I would always have Gabriel.

Bianca came to meet me a short time later. She was dressed in glowing orange silk that radiated like the sun. I had only seen one other woman wear orange, and on Bianca it was like an entirely different colour.

I smiled at her as she sat down by the window. "Isn't it

improper to outshine a bride on her wedding day."

"Believe me when I say it would be impossible. You look incredible, dear sister," Bianca replied.

"Thank you. Now, please do not take this the wrong way but I must ask. Is there anything I need to know before I meet the family?"

"Did you not ask my brother?"

"I know his answer already. Something along the lines of 'you have nothing to worry about, they will love you', and that is of no help to me at all."

"Well, in that case, where do I begin?" she started, staring at her hands as she thought. "My Mother may seem cold but she is not, she is just very guarded in unfamiliar surroundings. I am sure my brother told you that all of our powers are different. Some of us have better control than others. And, because of the nature of their powers, my sister Annalisa and my brother Matteo are fearful, not that Matteo would ever admit it. But what Annalisa has had to face at such a young age...."

"Can you tell me?"

"She inherited the ability to move objects with her mind from my Mother..."

"William can do that."

"Ah, but there is a difference. William needs a spell, Annalisa does not," she continued, and I felt myself blush. "Do not be embarrassed, it is a relevant comment. But that is not the issue. Annalisa is a necromancer, the first Santorini in two generations."

"What is a necromancer?"

"Someone who can communicate with the deceased and in some cases raise a body from the dead."

I gasped. "I can see why she would be frightened."

"Our grandmother said her aunt, who also had the power, eventually could not tell the difference between the dead and the living and she went mad. Silly woman started telling Annalisa this when she was three years old, it shouldn't be a huge shock that at age 13 she would be frightened beyond repair. Luckily she has six older siblings to help her, and now another sister who can see things from a different angle."

"I will do what I can to help any of you, I promise you that. But I am curious if a necromancer would have any control over vampires; the living dead, if you will."

"The topic has never presented itself, but it is a good question," she said, and before she could continue there was a sharp knock at the door. I glanced out the window, the sun had just set.

"Apparently destiny is ready for you," Bianca proclaimed. She checked herself in the mirror before heading for the door, Hannah was waiting. I nodded to them both as they turned to me, together we went downstairs.

Bianca went on ahead to be with the family. Most of the household was already gone. Vincenzo and Gabriel were waiting for me in the entry way. Tolone was doing a last minute check to make sure we had all we needed.

"You are a vision," Gabriel said as he embraced me, kissing both of my cheeks. "Your Grandmother is truly smiling from Heaven on this day."

"I wish she was here," I quietly told him.

"She is always with you, Katrine. Whether you like it or not." He smiled and winked at me.

Vincenzo took my hand then, and pulled me into his embrace. His warmth enveloped me and I instantly felt calmer.

"Is that part of your magic, mon ami?" I asked when he released me.

He smiled. "Only part, I assure you."

"Where is Gigi?" I asked. He seemed a bit shocked. "I may be angry with her but I would be crushed if..."

"I know. She left with Charles. You have nothing to worry about. Are you sure you are ready for this?"

"Of course."

"Morgana had a strange request. She asked that I ask you if you are wearing the dagger I gave you."

"Of course I am. After everything that has happened I would not go out without it."

Gabriel chuckled. "A dagger under your wedding dress? You truly are a Bathory."

"One can never be too careful," I replied. "Now, let's get moving. Wouldn't want to be late for my own wedding."

A MOMENT LIKE THIS

Gabriel took my arm as we walked in the front door of the church. I couldn't have asked for a more perfect location; a small, stone church just outside Paris, surrounded by beautiful, lush scenery. The sun had set and someone had lit torches, bathing everything in a warm glow.

"Hannah picked the location," Vincenzo said. "This is where the family always came, she said. I think her mother's funeral was here."

"So it is a sacred place," I replied. Vincenzo tried to move on ahead of us. "Where are you going?"

"I thought you were...," he began.

"I want you with me. If that is alright with Gabriel," I said, turning to my cousin.

Gabriel smiled. "I would expect nothing less."

Vincenzo blushed, it was the first time I had ever seen him do such a thing. He took my arm, and with him on my left and Gabriel on my right I felt as if I could take on the world.

We stepped into the main hall of the church and everyone stood. Wildflowers and red roses were everywhere, the smell perfuming the room and giving the impression we were not actually in a church.

I saw William standing at the front, when our eyes met I could not stop smiling. I was so happy to see him I practically pulled Vincenzo and Gabriel down the aisle.

A row full of people with stunning blue eyes was close to the front, the hair colour ranging in various shades of gold. An older man and woman stood next to each other, the woman smiled proudly at me and I could see William reflected back. I wondered if he had inherited his temper from his mother along with his looks.

Charles sat in the front row on the right side, Gigi, Morgana, Sybilla and Prince Radu next to him. He smiled warmly as Gigi dabbed her eyes with a handkerchief. Morgana appeared agitated, the expression on her face made the hair on the back of my neck stand up.

I pulled her to me and embraced her, whispering in her ear, "What have you seen?"

"Nothing, and that is the problem," she said sharply. "I have not had a vision in some time."

I pulled away from her, smiling awkwardly and trying not to attract attention. She nodded, as if signalling me not to be alarmed. Vincenzo embraced me, and then turned to say something to William.

Gabriel pulled me into his arms and we hugged each other tightly. Warmth spread from him to me, our heart beats felt as if they were joined together.

"I am so proud to be here with you. I never thought in a million years I would get to escort a bride on her wedding day," he said quietly to me as he stroked my hair.

"I would not be here without you. You are all I have of my family, and I am grateful to you in so many ways," I replied.

I gently kissed his cheek as he said, "Your Grandmother would be proud. I am sure she is smiling right now."

He took my hand and placed it in William's, wrapping both

his hands around ours.

"Many blessings on this most perfect union," Gabriel proclaimed and the room erupted in applause. He stepped away and took his seat beside Charles, the rest of the room sat as he did.

William and I stepped forward and kneeled before the priest, I kept a tight grip on his hand.

The priest preformed the ceremony in Latin, following the Catholic tradition. When he was done we were told to remain kneeling, and I was genuinely shocked when the priest left and Morgana took his place.

She lit a bundle of herbs with the flame from a nearby candle, blowing it so it was smoking. She walked around us, moving the herbs so the smoke made patterns, singing in a language I did not recognise. William handed her something and she continued on, stopping only to place a wreath on each of our heads.

She finally came to a stop, placing the herbs in a nearby dish so they could burn out, handing whatever it was back to William.

I smiled at her. "Thank you."

"Don't thank me. The Druid ceremony was his idea," she said, raising us up so we were standing.

William opened his hand to reveal a ring with tiny blue green stones. He slid it on to the third finger on my right hand, the room filled with happy cheers as he kissed me.

He and I had kissed many times before but it was nothing like this. This was the most perfect kiss; the symbol of the start of our union, of our commitment to each other. The moment when we officially became 'we'.

I took his face in my hands and the cheers continued. The day of being apart had made me miss him, all my fears and worries fell away as we stood and kissed.

"Hello wife," he said when we finally came apart.

I could not help but smile. "Hello husband."

"I never thought we would get to this place."

I touched his face again, rubbing my thumb along his chin. He closed his eyes and eased in to my touch.

"Now you know not to doubt me when I am determined."

He laughed loudly and pulled me into a hug. "Did Morgana have any predictions for our marriage?"

"Apparently she hasn't had a vision for some time," I said, he pulled away from me to stare at my face.

That is when I smelt the smoke.

Our guests began to frantically move around the church, trying to find a way out but all the doors and windows were locked.

William and I went to the main doors and I noticed something dangling from the knob.

"Could that priest have done this? Discovered what we are and decided to burn us?" William asked as I moved slowly towards the door. It appeared to be a necklace, and when I picked it up and examined it I discovered it was stones that looked like the eyes of a cat. An image of a ring with a similar stone flashed in my mind and I gasped.

"What is that?" William said sharply.

"We have to get out of here," I said, moving back into the main room. Someone had smashed a window and people were climbing out of it. William pulled me towards his family, who seemed oddly calm.

"Can you go out and see what we are dealing with, Matteo?" William asked his brother, who looked like an older version of him. Matteo nodded, and walked through one of the outer walls as if he was passing through an open doorway.

"Bianca, can you try to put the fire out?" William continued, and he gave his family specific jobs in quick and perfect Italian. His other brother Gianni and his father Davide went out the window with the others while his mother Luciana and his sisters Gemma and Carlotta went to the front doors to try to get them open.

Which left Annalisa, the youngest, who Bianca had spoke to me about with me. I took the girl's hand; her expression was blank except the fear that sparkled in her eyes.

"You look very pretty in your dress," I said to her in Italian, smiling as warmly as I could considering the circumstances. "I did not know I was getting such a lovely little sister."

She smiled. She had lovely straight white teeth. Her gold hair was swept high and off her face in an elegant updo.

"You're safe with us, bambina," William told her. "Hold Katrine's hand so you don't get lost."

I had never felt such power like what I felt when I took the little girl's hand.

Matteo came back through the wall and headed to us. "There's a group of people. I see fighting. They appear to be led by a blonde woman. She is fighting with the French woman."

"Do the two women look similar?" I asked.

He furrowed his brow as if he was annoyed that I had interrupted him. "I could not tell. It was dark. But it did look like the other woman had lost part of her nose."

Luciana Santorini yelled a warning to her children as the front doors blew open.

It was the Cesari.

A hot wave of anger washed through me as I fiddled with the necklace that I gripped tightly in my left hand.

They were attacking on my wedding day.

I started for the doors, my anger driving me forward. Annalisa came right along beside me, William close at her heels.

We stepped out into the darkness to a battlefield. Our people were fighting with the Cesari, who seemed only to be trying to get them out of the way so they could attack my new family.

I scanned the crowd and quickly spotted Gigi, deep in combat with a blonde woman whose face was hidden by darkness.

But I did not have time to study her, because as soon as Annalisa and I were visible all attention turned to us.

Knowing what I did about her powers it made sense that witch hunters would come after her. She was the most dangerous.

I started casting every spell I could think of to keep people away from us. Between William and I we seemed to have it covered.

Luciana and I made eye contact as she, Gemma and Carlotta raced out into the fight. I tried to reassure her with my gaze that I would do my best to protect her youngest and my husband, her third son.

William moved us away from the doors to make room for Bianca. She had somehow used her powers to gain control of the fire, it pooled around her ankles like water and sparked in her hands as she moved her fingers. I suddenly became quite nervous for those of us who could be hurt by fire, especially Gabriel.

But that little girl's hand tightly gripping mine gave me focus. I blocked out the hideous screams, and the visions of my past.

I jumped back as the fire streamed past, pushing Annalisa behind me. Bianca stepped down into the fight as the church collapsed behind her, throwing us on to the grass. I could not hold back my tears any longer as I watched all of Hannah's work, her sacred place, went up in flames.

But I had to reassure myself she would be alright and focus on the task at hand.

Bianca made short work of a number of our attackers, and it appeared they were retreating. We kept back and out of the direct fighting; a blood curdling wail caught my attention and turned my head.

Gigi collapsed in a heap, and I caught a brief glimpse of

blonde hair as her attacker ran off with the others.

I watched and waited with baited breath for Gigi to get up. I prayed silently to whoever might be listening but she remained on the ground. Vincenzo ran to her and I struggled to contain my screams.

It was as if time slowed, agonising as I handed Annalisa to William, pointed at Gigi and ran.

The blade had been plunged into her stomach all the way to the hilt with blood spreading out from the wound. Vincenzo had pulled her into his lap as she sobbed. Her beautiful face and dressed were ruined with streaks of bright red blood.

"Who did this to you Gigi?" I asked.

She turned to me and coughed, and I knew with just a look.

"She knew," her voice was hoarse. "She knew if she attacked him you would want to marry him and it would draw them out. She said she needed them. She needed them and me."

"The whole thing was a trap? She used my wedding day as a trap?"

She coughed again, sputtering blood, pulling in laboured short breaths. "I am so sorry ma petite."

"We have to do something!" I exclaimed. I stood, preparing to scream for help when I noticed the bodies.

The fighting had stopped, and now the grass was littered with bodies.

"Are you alright, my love?" William ran over to me, hanging on to Annalisa. "You're bleeding!"

I looked down, it appeared I had touched Gigi's wound and it was all over my fingers and stained the necklace I still had in my hands. Some blood had even got on my wedding ring.

"I'm fine. It's Gigi," I said flatly. "Are you two unharmed?"

"A bit shook up but physically fine," he replied, looking down at his little sister. Now when I saw her face she appeared her age of 13 years.

"Can you help Gigi?" I asked him.

"We can try."

I felt the hot tears run down my cheek. I gulped in air as if I was choking.

"I am going to look for Morgana," I mumbled. I touched his face, kissing his lips gently. "I won't be long. Stay here please."

He nodded and I went off to look for some help.

I found Prince Radu and Sybilla standing off to the side, covered in blood.

"My daughter fought well," Radu stated to me. "Do not worry. The blood is not ours."

"Please help the injured, if you can. I need Morgana," I said.

"The Druid? What on earth for?"

"Grisela is badly hurt."

Sybilla reached out her hand to me and touched my fingers. "Aseem is protecting the other humans. We will send him to her at once."

"Thank you," I said and continued on.

I tried not to look at the bodies. A loud wail stopped me dead in my tracks; a mother's pained cries. Someone in William's family had been hurt or worse.

"Morgana!" I called out. Everyone turned but I still couldn't find her. I stood where I was, hoping she would find me if I stayed in the same place and called her name.

Aseem ran past, heading for Gigi.

The relief was only momentary, even when Morgana finally appeared.

"You saw none of this," I said, a statement instead of a question.

"None," she replied.

"Are you hurt?"

"No."

"Have you seen Hannah? Or Gabriel?"

"The humans stayed together, protected each other. Your Gabriel fought with honour, like the great general I am sure he was...is...I do not know how this works. I have not seen such bloodshed in a long time. It is doing strange things to my mind."

"Gigi is badly hurt. Please go to her," I said, and I pointed her in the right direction. Gabriel appeared, like a beacon of light in the heavy darkness, his mouth rimmed with blood and a dripping sword dragging beside him.

I had a vision of him as he once was, the great Prince. He saw me and something flickered in his eyes, as if he had seen someone else before he had seen me.

"Are you hurt?" I asked him when he was close enough to hear me.

He smiled, the look was unsettling. "No, and I must apologise. I've found the action exhilarating. Are you well, my sweet?"

"Not hurt, but not well," I began, I had started crying again. "This massacre, on my wedding day! There is a blade in Gigi's stomach...so many fallen! I have not seen Hannah, or Charles. My God! Where is Charles?"

"I do not know, but let us tend to Grisela first. I am assuming your husband is fine as well?"

"And Vincenzo. They are with Gigi."

"Then we should go to her, assess the damage, and then check the other soldiers."

"How can you be so calm?"

He hesitated. "I apologise, I suppose I am thinking like a general."

"Perhaps that is best," I said. He followed behind as I started back to Gigi.

Bianca stepped into our path, the fire still swimming around her. "This isn't over. Follow me."

ASHES

Bianca said nothing as she stalked off towards the wooded area, Gabriel and I kept a safe distance behind.

I could not bring myself to ask her what happened; she'd told me before that she would burn Paris to the ground if something happened to William.

She was my sister now. I would help her in any way I could.

Shadows moved quickly in the darkness among the trees as we approached. I tried to use my senses but all I could get was fear.

Bianca moved at a measured pace as we walked through the trees, as we moved I could feel the presence of others, some standing still and others running in fright.

There was several hiding behind trees around us. I assumed hoping we would not notice. I waited for Bianca to move ahead, and then signalled Gabriel that they were close. He nodded, charging off on his own in one direction as I went in another.

The first didn't see me coming. I reached around the side of the tree and grabbed a handful of hair, yanking forward until they were in my grasp. There was some flailing, and a fist that missed my jaw by mere inches. That movement gave me the opportunity to pull them up and sink my teeth into where the neck connected to the shoulder.

I bit down hard, my mouth open as wide as I could manage, and tore a hunk of flesh out. The body convulsed for only a moment before going slack, hanging limply by the hair I still firmly gripped in my hand.

I spat the flesh out, blood coating the inside of my mouth. I shook the body where it hung, simply to check if it was dead, tossed it aside and kept moving.

The more blood I had the faster I moved. Quickly they caught on and started to run, and soon enough Gabriel and I were back together with Bianca just up ahead.

She had a person in each hand, gripping their throats tightly as their skin burned and bubbled, peeling away and flaking off into the wind like ashes.

A group began to advance on us, pulling swords to try to attack Bianca. I used one of my spells to push them back; some stumbled while others flung quite a distance backwards.

Gabriel swung his sword, decapitating an attacker with one swing. He was incredible with a weapon. I would have to ask him to teach me.

A blast of fire exploded in front of me, Bianca had caught three as they were coming at me.

Off in the distance I caught a glimpse of a woman watching us, a light blonde plait peeking out from the hood of her cloak.

I signalled Bianca and she sent a fireball blazing towards the woman, the trees and people who stood in its path exploding into ash. The woman had vanished, but if I had learned anything from all of this it certainly did not mean she was gone.

Someone flew at me, knocking me off my feet. We wrestled, rolling around on the ground as I tried to feel something to use as a weapon.

But I was not fast enough, and I screamed as the blade sunk into my shoulder.

"That was for Colombina," my attacker growled in Italian, the fact that the voice was female gave it a strange pitch.

I slammed my forehead into her nose, the shower of blood splattering on my face as she fell back.

"You can't kill me that easily," I snapped, she seemed shocked I could speak her language so well. I pulled the blade out of my shoulder, and then used my hand to hold her face to the ground.

"This is for the Santorini," I said, then shoved the blade into her ear canal, leaning into it when it became harder to push.

I pulled the blade back out when the body stopped twitching. My shoulder ached when I moved.

I stood and assessed my surroundings. We appeared to be the only ones left standing. Bianca's fire was beginning to dwindle.

"Is it done?" I asked Bianca.

"For now. We will leave the rest for the wolves," she said, turning and heading back without another word.

I leaned against a tree, pausing for a moment to try to catch my breath.

Gabriel reached out and took my free arm. "Why do you have that necklace around your wrist?"

I looked at him and my arm. I must have put the necklace around my wrist during the fight. He put my arm around his neck and held me tightly by the waist for support as we walked together back towards the others.

The Santorini were gathered together, Luciana was kneeling down beside three bodies with a fourth cradled in her arms. William saw us, called my name and ran from his family.

"You're bleeding," he touched his fingers to my shoulder.

"Bianca needed me," I said.

Gabriel transferred me into William's arms while saying,

"You're family now. We always support our family."

"Thank you," William replied, clutching Gabriel's hand for a moment. The two men nodded to each other, I suppose as recognition of service.

"Please go check on Gigi," I said to Gabriel. He nodded and went without a word.

"That's what she stabbed me with," I told William as he took the blade from my hand. "You were right about Colombina. I thought I should take it in case I got sick or something."

"Your attacker is dead?" he asked. I gave him an angry look and he rolled his eyes. "I'm sorry I asked, I should have known better."

"How is Annalisa?" I asked as we slowly started towards his family.

"Frightened but well."

"And the rest of your family?"

His expression darkened. "My father is hurt. One brother is dead and the other dying. My sister Gemma went quickly, her defensive spells weren't strong enough. But they had been after her for years."

"Gigi said this was all a trap. Your kidnapping, everything. All to get your family in the same place. All because they needed something."

"I am so sorry, my love. If I'd had any notion..."

"No, William. If I had not pushed, if I had not been so..."

He pulled me to him, hugging me tightly to his body. "This is the curse of my kind. As long as we are, there will be those who hunt us."

"So we'll just have to kill them all," I stated as we continued on to his family.

I knelt down beside Luciana, who held her dying son Matteo in her lap. He had walked through walls not that long ago.

I touched his hand and got shocked, a wave of electricity shot through my system. I could still feel it in my veins after I took my hand away.

He chuckled, coughing slightly, causing blood to ooze from his wounds. He said something that sounded like 'Good Luck' in Italian, and then turned his eyes back to his mother.

"I am so sorry," I said to Luciana in Italian. My tears started again and I felt myself blush from embarrassment. She watched me with a confused expression, as if she did not quite understand what I was doing. She looked up at William who was standing behind me for some guidance.

"She feels responsible," William said so quickly I barely understood him.

"By loving my son you have become part of this fight. This was happening long before you came along. You are not in any way responsible," she said sharply. "Your people have suffered because of us."

"They are as much a part of William and I as you are. We would fight for each other...," I began, stopping when she recoiled back in shock. I heard her whisper 'lupo' and the others began to huddle together in fear.

I turned to find two wolves limping towards me; the white wolf's coat was stained pink with blood, the darker wolf came closer to me and smelt my shoulder.

"It's alright. They're with us," I told Luciana, then turned back to the darker wolf. "I was worried."

The wolf made a rumbling noise that sounded like a chuckle. He nudged me with his nose and I scratched behind his ears.

"Where is Natalia?" I asked the wolf. He lay down beside me and curled up into a ball. "Charles, please. I am being serious."

The white wolf began to circle around us as if she was patrolling, coming back once in a while to sniff Charles.

"I think he is hurt much worse than it looks," William said quietly as he sat down beside me.

"Why would you say that?" I asked.

"Because Mathilde is not one to be protective of Charles," he said. Bianca suddenly stood and started to pace. She wiggled her fingers at her sides which created sparks of electricity.

"I am going to dispose of the bodies," she mumbled.

"Only Cesari," William told her. "We will give the others a proper burial."

She mumbled something else then left. I hadn't heard what she said, but I wondered if it had something to do with most of our people not being able to really die.

"She and I will be head of the family now. It comes with certain responsibilities," William quietly told me. Luciana sighed loudly and stroked Matteo's head, only when I saw a tear fall on her cheek did I realise he had died.

"Is he safe?" Annalisa's little voice was quiet as she stood beside me, leaning over my shoulder so she could look at Charles.

"Yes! Do not worry," I said, and I scratched behind one of Charles's ears and said to him, "Charles, there is a young lady here who would like to meet you."

He stuck up his head and I brought Annalisa's hand forward so he could sniff it.

"Charles, this is William's youngest sister, Annalisa," I said, and the wolf crawled forward so the little girl could pet him. "Annalisa, this is Charles, Lord Westwick. He is the leader of the Danse Macabre."

She said one of several words for werewolf in Italian and sat down beside me to pet him. Seeing how pleased she was gave me a few moments of peace.

I watched Charles and wondered what must be going on in his mind. While I was pleased he would take the time and amuse the frightened girl we needed to regroup and get back to the chateau.

But why did it fall on him to take charge?

And with that thought Victorie appeared, blood was smeared on her face. Her hair had fallen loose; her hands were crusted with dirt and blood.

"We have to go," she came to stand in front of us, I wasn't sure if she was speaking to me or Charles.

"We need carriages, and a way to carry...," I began.

"We have four. I apologise, William, but your family will have to ride with the dead," she said.

"That is not a problem," William replied.

"I am sending those who have to avoid the sun ahead with the injured," Victorie continued. "William's family goes after them, then the rest of us."

"Katrine is injured," William proclaimed.

Victorie started peculiarly at me. "I can see that. You will go with the injured."

"No," I snapped. Charles growled at me.

"We will be right behind you," William said quietly to me. He helped me to my feet and I suddenly felt light-headed.

"She's losing blood," William told Victorie.

She stuck her hand out to me and I took it, stepping over Charles.

I looked down at the wolf and said, "You will protect them?"

He grunted and Victorie held tightly to my hand.

"Do not worry. You have my word," Victorie said.

"We're right behind you," William called as Victorie lead me away.

Gabriel gathered me up in his arms and helped me into the carriage, we were tightly packed in. Gigi lay on the floor, unconscious. Her breathing was shallow. I watched her as we got moving, worried that the bumpy ride would somehow hurt her.

I was so afraid for her and what would happen to her that I began to sob uncontrollably. Gabriel pulled me closer to his body to muffle my wailing.

When, if, she wakes, I would find out who did this to her and I would hunt them to the ends of the earth. Not only for what they had done to her but for what they had done to my new family.

But I could think of nothing else in that moment other than crying. Gabriel silently held me as I cried all the way back to the chateau.

AWAKENING

My shoulder throbbed and burned at the same time, any sort of movement sent what felt like sparks shooting through my body.

I spent my wedding night in a heavy haze, and when I opened my eyes the next morning the grogginess that weighed me down made me wonder what they'd put in my tea last night. I was angry.

"Relax, my love," William's soothing voice seemed to surround me, but as my eyes opened and closed I could not focus on his face.

"Why did you drug me?" I asked.

"You're hurt and you need to rest," Morgana said angrily.

I rolled slightly and winced in pain. "Gigi."

"She's well taken care of." Morgana's tone was beyond anger. "And, Lord help me, if you get out of this bed before you have healed..."

"We have to....I need to...."

"You *need* to rest before you get yourself killed!" she yelled. "You are not a one woman army!"

I groaned in pain. "Gabriel..."

"I'm here!" he called from somewhere in the room.

"The Order...Countess Zrinyi....," I began, the fuzz in my head clouding my thoughts. A soft hand touched my head and slowly stroked my hair. Someone had removed the pearls while I was asleep.

"Please," I said quietly. "I won't get up, but I don't want to sleep anymore. I don't like this feeling..."

"Drugging her may have been excessive," William said. My eyes were too heavy to stay open.

"You did not see how she was when you were kidnapped," Vincenzo's voice was clear and sharp. "She was not hurt then, and with the extent of Gigi's injuries it's best for her to recover before she goes looking for vengeance."

"Has Gigi said anything more?" William asked.

"No. She's been unconscious since last night," Vincenzo paused, and then said quietly. "The blade may have been poisoned or had some sort of spell or potion on it."

My body clenched and William pulled me into his arms. He had been stroking my hair. Tears started to edge their way out from my closed eyelids.

"Drugging doesn't do much good when *she can hear you!*" Morgana yelled.

"Alright! Everyone *leave! Now!*" William said. I could hear the frustration in his voice. I wanted to tell him to go be with his family, that I was sufficiently drugged that I would not be leaving this bed without help. I would be alright while he attended to their needs.

"I know what you are thinking Katrine, and you can just forget it. My mother would never forgive me if I left you," he said. "Now sleep, my love. Trust me. It can wait."

The next time I woke the fog had passed and I rose with a clear head. I pushed myself up into a sitting position. A dull throb pulsed from my shoulder.

"Hello wife," William said. We were in his chamber; he was

sitting at his desk.

"Hello husband," I replied, my voice was hoarse, my throat dry. He pointed at the table by the bedside where a pitcher of water and a mug sat.

I poured, pausing before I drank. "Is this drugged?"

He chuckled. "No." He let out a deep breath, and then continued. "That was mostly Vincenzo and Morgana's idea. You can blame them if you feel the need to be angry."

I gulped back two mugs of water and still did not feel fulfilled.

"Will you take me to see Gigi?" I asked him.

"There is not much to see. She is still unconscious," he replied.

"For how long?"

"A full day."

"So I have only missed one day?"

He smiled. "Yes. Do not worry."

"I am sorry I slept through our wedding night. And I am sorry that I have to insist you send for some blood."

He laughed, lifting a canister off the desk and bringing it along as he came to sit with me. He sat on top of the blankets at first, until I pulled them back and he crawled in beside me after removing his shoes.

"Did you undo my hair?" I asked him. "And put me in a clean shift?"

I looked down at what I was wearing; it was the wedding nightgown Hannah had been embroidering. I was terrified to ask if my wedding dress had survived.

"Hannah and Morgana cleaned you up and dressed your wound," he said. I took the canister from him and quickly emptied it.

"More?" he asked when I handed it back.

"Maybe after I see Gigi," I tried to get up and he stopped me.

"Katrine, I don't think it is wise," he said. "You have been through enough. Someone will send word if there is any change."

"Do I need to obey your commands now?"

"Pardon me if I do not want your heart broken further." He did not bother hiding his anger. "If you really want to watch her lying in a bed, go ahead. But I won't join you. I've had enough."

He went to stand and I pulled him back down. "I am sorry, William. This is not easy for me. Have you been to check on your family?"

"That is something I need to speak to you about," he began. "We have been asked to return to Naples to help bury the dead. And Vincenzo thinks it would be a good time for us to go find the blood cure. He thinks it would help Gigi."

"Is it wise for us to travel together after what has happened? Especially if it was all a plot? And this evil that keeps getting talked about, I am not sure we should separate."

"Only Gigi said..."

"But does it not make sense? Can you not see it? I mean, really think about all that has happened, and if *she* was helping them..."

"Who do you mean *she*?"

I could not help but huff loudly. "We found Beatrix's seal when we found you. And when Gigi was attacked I saw..."

"Did you see Beatrix's face?" he asked. "Even if you did it doesn't change much. A plan has been made. We just needed to decide what route to follow."

"What is this 'plan'?"

"We shall separate for a while, to explore our options. Then, as a group, we shall decide what path to take."

"And this means what exactly?"

"Some of us shall go look for the blood cure, some shall stay in Paris. There was some talk of a group going into Spain, but they may wait until we return. We have to assess the threat and decide how best to deal with it. I think Les Vieux will be sticking around for assistance, and Gabriel wants to speak to the Order."

"We are splitting up?"

He stroked my hair. "No, no. We are just going to do some

scouting and see if we should relocate. And several blood drinkers, Gigi included, were badly injured. Vincenzo has information that has led him to believe the blood cure could help her."

"So, who stays and who goes?"

"Apparently Charles has decided now is a good time for him to finally, and fully, take the lead. He will ultimately make those decisions."

I laughed, which caused my shoulder to ache. "Let us pray he does not only think of himself for once. He cannot possibly think I would allow him to go search for the blood cure and leave Gigi here alone and unprotected."

"Sweetheart, I fear there are some things about this situation you are failing to understand."

"And what is that, my love?"

"You will have no input or say in how this goes. You have no authority, neither do I for that matter. It may not appear that way but there is a group of elders within the Danse Macabre that aids Charles in these situations. He calls them his 'generals'."

"I can't believe I did not know about this until now," I said quietly. "So who are they, and who shall we follow?"

"We shall follow Vincenzo. He will need us for trading and communicating with people along the way, and he has asked that we join him. As I said previously, we shall take my family back to Naples then be on our way. I am part of this trade business and he wishes to include you so it makes logical sense." He paused for a moment before continuing. "These generals are Vincenzo, Victorie, Mathilde, Tommas and Gigi. There was another but he died some time ago. I believe Victorie will join us, Mathilde may go to Spain and Charles will stay here."

I stayed silent, allowing everything he had just told me to mull over in my mind. I had been told many times that my behaviour would not always be accepted. I knew the time would come eventually.

Too many people had got hurt because I had rushed in

without thinking. Perhaps I should let someone else make the plans and the decisions for a while.

"Could we go to Spain another time?" I asked. He paused, as if he was confused.

His fingers ran gently through my hair. "Of course. I do believe this little expedition will be quite fantastic, and we shall see some wonders beyond anything you could imagine."

"I'm sure it will be wonderful."

He pulled me closer to him and kissed me, passion and energy bursting forth and drawing us into each other. My hand explored his body as his explored mine. Our new status gave us freedom that drew a new energy, a wave of emotion that had us close to tearing at each other.

His hand gently cupped my breast over my shift; he ran the pad of his thumb over my nipple sending a shutter throughout my body.

I pulled his shirt off over his head and ran my hands over his muscular chest, my fingers learning each line and curve as if studying a map for the first time.

Slowly we both explored each other's bodies, and soon enough we lay naked in each other's arms. Before I could think about being embarrassed he had pulled me tightly to him, his fingers gently moving down my body until they reached my lady parts. I could feel his member swelling against my leg as his fingers began to stroke me, my breath quickened as I began to tingle.

He pulled away from me for only a moment, a small gasp escaping from my mouth. "Are you sure you want to do this? Are ready for this?" he asked.

"I am. Just remember to be gentle. This is my first time," I said.

"You may not believe me but it is my first time as well," he replied as he kissed down my neck. "If it hurts too much please say something."

I nodded and his mouth met mine as he moved his body in

between my legs. In one swift motion he slid his member inside me, the initial sharp pain replaced by a wave of pleasure.

We began to move together, the more motion we made the faster the pain was gone and replaced with sensitivity and delight. I moaned and writhed as we kissed, his breath catching in his throat with each thrust.

My body began to clench as the emotions began to swell, his pace sped up and we went to the brink together, my fingers dug into his shoulders as we both climaxed.

We collapsed in a heap of sweaty limbs, tangled together with the sheets stuck to our bodies.

"Did I hurt you?" he whispered in my ear, his hot breath giving me the shivers.

"No. But I suspect our bed linens will need to be changed," I replied. His laughter sent a vibration through both our bodies, as if we had merged into one.

He softly kissed my cheek. "I love you, Katrine. Despite all that happened, our wedding was one of the greatest moments of my life."

"I love you too, William. And no matter what you thought of my early motivations, marrying you was the best decision I've ever made. I am the luckiest girl in the world."

THE VOW

I snuck out of bed later that night while William was sleeping. The chateau was dark and quiet so I had no problem getting to Gigi's room unnoticed.

A sliver of moonlight was all I had to guide me as I crept into Gigi's room, her curtains loosely drawn. She lay sleeping peacefully in her bed, her blonde hair spread out on the pillow around her. She looked like an angel.

I knelt down beside her and took her hand. It was cold.

"I don't know if you can hear me," I began quietly. "But I swear to you that I will do whatever I can to make you better. I will find the cure for whatever this is and give you your life back."

The moonlight from the window shifted, the lace curtain pattern filling the room with shapes and designs.

"And if *she* did this," I squeezed her hand in frustration, "if Beatrix did this she will die by my hand, and next time I won't assume. I won't stop until I know she has taken her last breath. She will pay for everything she has done to us in this life and the next, I swear it. I don't even care why she's done these things anymore. There is talk of great evil, but it doesn't matter to me."

I wiped the tears from my face with the back of my hand. "I

am going on a journey with Vincenzo and I will have to leave you in the care of other people. I don't like it but I'm going to have to trust they have your best interests at heart. I am going to have to trust Charles with your care...but you two were in love once. I hope that would be enough for him to do the right thing. He has proven himself lately...."

I chuckled to myself, the tears coming more steadily now. Charles was a good man, even though he occasionally did questionable things. I began to laugh; it was rather amusing to think about the human flaws of someone not so human.

Perhaps there was not that much of a separation. We were not as damned as I had thought.

"Vincenzo thinks he may have found something that could help you so we are going to retrieve it. Also they're talking of sending a group to Spain as a possible place to relocate." I explained. "Could you imagine? I have never been to Spain, perhaps we could go to a coastal town where it's warm. I know your heart is in Paris but I think it would grow on you. Especially somewhere without snow." I took in a shallow breath. "Oh, Gigi, I never thought I would go anywhere without you! Even though I will have Vincenzo and my husband I am petrified....I won't even get into my fears about having a husband. I know you may not understand why I did what I did, but I am happy I married him and would not change a thing. I even would have done it had you not dismissed me."

Gigi's fingers felt cold and dead in my hand. There seemed to be nothing coming from her, no life force radiating, no essential energy pulsing through her even though she lay motionless. It was as if her body was an empty shell. I could not help but wonder if it would all be for nothing, if she was already long gone.

"I won't give up," I said, kissing her icy fingers. "You can count on me. You won't regret bringing me into the fold, I swear. I will fix this. You have my word."

I lay her hand gently on the bed, stroking her hand before I stood. I left the room without another word, quietly closing the door and going back to our room without looking back.

"Katrine," a voice called from the end of the hallway, a dim light shone through the open library door.

"How is she?" Victorie asked as I stepped in the room. She was leaning over the desk, pouring over several maps she'd spread out over the surface. A large bowl of water sat off to one side.

"Cold," I replied.

She sighed loudly, the candlelight illuminating the scar on her face.

"I hope that it will not stop you from coming on this journey with us," she continued. "We could really use you."

"I will do what I can."

"I will be leading part of the expedition, I have journeyed these lands before. Are you comfortable with me taking the lead?"

I smiled. "It would be nice, for a change."

"Good! I am so pleased. I hope you will encourage the Scots.... pardon me. I hope you will encourage Morgana to come along. Vincenzo may believe he and William can handle the magical aspects of this journey on their own but I do not agree. I will ask her personally, but I hope you will as well," she said. She stood fully, giving off quite the regal impression. She spoke like she was dictating plans to her military. It made me wonder what she had experienced in her long life.

"I will most definitely. Now, if you'll excuse me, I need to get some sleep," I replied.

"Of course. Good night, Katrine. I look forward to getting to know you better on this journey."

"And I as well, Victorie. Perhaps one day you will tell me about Alienor."

YSABEAU

Fall 1615

The journey was long, far longer than she had expected. Eduardo had insisted that she rode in a carriage, like a proper lady, and he rode alongside her on his glorious white stallion. She watched him through the window, she was afraid to be outside the chateau without him.

But she was going to stay with her mother now. The queen was dead and it was time for her fostering to end.

She had written to her mother weeks ago to ask if Eduardo could stay with them. He had been her constant companion, her knight, her guardian, for her entire life and the idea of losing him in this next phase of her life made her nauseous.

"How much longer?" she called out to him. "This is madness. Why could I not have ridden my horse?"

"We are approaching the gates of Paris, child. It won't be much longer now. And I would not want your mother to think that you were not properly cared for all this time," he replied, riding ahead a bit so she couldn't ask any more questions.

Ysabeau sat back with a huff. She was old enough that she

should be able to make such decisions for herself. She was in her twelfth year. She could be married now depending on what her mother decided.

Perhaps she would finally get to meet her father. Her mother did live with him. It was only inevitable.

They rode for a little while longer, and then the carriage finally came to a stop. Ysabeau inhaled deeply, and tried to appear calm when Eduardo opened the door.

"Your mother knows you are coming, child," Eduardo said, holding out his hand. "There is no need to be so nervous."

"But what if she does not approve of me?" she asked, looking up at him when she stepped out on the sidewalk. She looked up the large chateau that loomed ahead of her.

"You are everything anyone could hope for in a daughter, Ysabeau. You will do fine. Just remember what I taught you," he said, taking her arm and escorting her up the stairs. He stood back from her a bit after he knocked hard on the door.

A maid answered, smiling brightly and looking down at Ysabeau. "May I help you?"

"I am looking for Mademoiselle Grisela Delphine. She is expecting me," Ysabeau proclaimed.

The maid shifted back and forth on her feet uncomfortably, her face looked confused.

"Is something wrong?" Ysabeau asked. Butterflies began to dance in her stomach.

"Please come in," the maid ushered them in to the entryway, then disappeared. Ysabeau reached out for Eduardo and he held the girl's arm protectively.

The maid returned with a beautiful dark haired young woman, and a tall thin man with piercing green eyes. The woman looked Ysabeau up and down; the young girl could do nothing but stare back.

"You are looking for Mademoiselle Delphine? I am her protégée, Katrine Bathory, and this is our associate Signor Amori," the dark haired woman began. "How may I help you?"

Ysabeau's eyes filled with tears. "She is expecting me. Did she tell no one I was coming?"

"May I ask your name, child?"

Ysabeau took a deep breath. "My name is Ysabeau. I am Mademoiselle Delphine's daughter."

Signor Amori began to laugh, but Katrine Bathory put her hand on his arm and silenced him. He looked to her for an explanation and she nodded, his eyes grew wide.

"It is an honour to finally meet you, Ysabeau. Please do not worry, you are safe here," Katrine moved closer to the girl. "I am afraid your mother is ill and has been sleeping for some time. But we will take care of you for the time being."

"Are you inviting in strangers without my permission, Mademoiselle Bathory?" a well dressed man with dark hair and a sharp gaze moved in between them and approached Eduardo. "I am Lord Charles Westwick, the leader of the Danse Macabre. And who are you?"

"My name is Ysabeau," the young girl proclaimed. "I am Grisela Delphine's daughter. And I believe you may be my father."

EPILOGUE

The night had enveloped her, her features hidden under the shadow cast by the hood of her cloak. Darkness had become a part of her being. She existed within it now, as if she was made from shadows. The cold night had sunk into her bones, changing her in ways she had never dreamed possible but felt right for her body.

As if all of this had been fate. Kismet. Destiny. What he had spoke of so long ago.

She had not thought of his face in many moons. Now it came to her as if she had seen it mere moments before; handsome and young, like a statue.

She wondered if she could find her, find Anastasia. The daughter she never knew, that never knew her. *Their* daughter. If they could be together in this life they had been cast into, like stones skipping across a pond.

But she was no longer as she once was. Would she want her now that she was no longer The Countess, but just Erzsebet?

She could not help but wonder if all that had transpired was to bring her to this place. Was for her to defy death and continue to live free of the binds that had once confined her, mortal bonds that she felt little for now. Perhaps it would not be wise to seek out the anchors to her old life, but start anew.

What does one who cheated death call themselves?

ACKNOWLEDGMENTS

A big theme of this book is not allowing fear to stop you from doing things - which is exactly the reason why it took so long for this book to come out. The list of fears is too many to name. I realized that all my fears were doing was holding the story back, and that's not fair to the characters and the people who love them.

So, here we are.

I would like to thank my father, Lawrence Maurice, for helping bring this book together. For always giving me new ideas, and for the encouragement.

I would also like to thank Sheila Carmichael, for always believing in my stories, and in me. And one of the illustrious 'Ladies Who Lunch', Dorothy, for the inspiration for Eduardo, and allowing me to pay respects to his namesake. I am truly sorry for your loss, and I hope I have done him some justice.

I also have to thank RM Gilmore for her fantastic design work, and for helping make my words look amazing. And of course for being a great friend. Rebirth is all the more special because it was the beginning of our collaborations. I look forward to many more.

And as always my husband and daughter. I have to thank them for being a great family.

I never thought when I started this series that my Mom would not be there when it came to a close. It's a weird feeling.

But this is not the forever end. This is just the 'for now' end. So, in the words of The Simpsons, I won't say goodbye just smell you later.

www.ingramcontent.com/pod-product-compliance
Lightning Source LLC
Chambersburg PA
CBHW071527110726
47908CB00003B/966